A DAY IN THE SECTION

Jay Bhatti

gatekeeper press™
Tampa, Florida

The views and opinions expressed in this book are solely those of the author and do not necessarily reflect the views or opinions of Gatekeeper Press. Gatekeeper Press is not to be held responsible for and expressly disclaims responsibility of the content herein.

A Day in The Section

Published by Gatekeeper Press
7853 Gunn Hwy, Suite 209
Tampa, FL 33626
www.GatekeeperPress.com

Library of Congress Control Number: 2021940578

ISBN (paperback): 9781662915840
eISBN: 9781662915857

Dedicated to everyone who dreams of the impossible, let this novel be a testament to its reality. Never stop pursuing your passion, no matter what anyone says to you, especially yourself.

Introduction

Like anything in my life, it always starts with some random idiotic idea. This one was about an ex-agent sneaking around and murdering people in London while a rookie agent tried to stop him. As it seemed like a fantastic idea to see as a film, I jotted a brief outline of what it could be. It's something I tend to do with anything that captures my attention for more than fifteen minutes. However, in mapping it out, I had this crazy notion that maybe this would work much better as a novel.

Once that played in my mind, I honestly asked, *"Yeah, why not?"* Of course, I've never created anything remotely like that, but "why not?" Even if it were to only stay as some random word document on my hard drive for decades, no one would ever know about. Like every other short film, TV show and film script I've ever written or started to write.

Still, I was intrigued by this idea and genuinely wanted to know if I could write something like this. So, after weeks of writing, I drafted the entire story from start to finish. It was extremely basic, with almost no punctuation or character, but it made me think more than any other idea I had. So, many months later, needing a distraction between working at Volvo, editing what would eventually turn out to be my award-winning short film, and recording hundreds of film reviews, I decided to keep playing around with it. With each revised draft, this nifty idea of mine kept getting more compelling, more fascinating, hypnotising me even more.

Once I had that encouragement in myself, I pressed on, shaping and moulding it. I wrote new chapters, throwing out old ones and removing crap ideas. I gave these characters a sense of life, a personality, and a purpose that people would hopefully identify with throughout the novel.

Then many, many more months later, after another two dozen or so drafts, I reached the point where I felt like it's something I honestly think people would enjoy reading. So after that, I set out to get it published. Then after another year and a half of fine-tuning every paragraph, sentence and word, I finished it. I'd finally finished the entire piece, from start to finish, and I couldn't be prouder of what I wrote.

So, now that this arduous process is finally over for me, I leave it to you, the random person who picked up a copy of my novel. I hope you enjoy it, whether it's a physical copy or an electronic version. I wish that from the first page until the end, you find it as gripping and enjoyable to read as I did to write. And think that this random author you'd never heard of wrote something pretty brilliant, and are glad you took the time to read it.

It's something that will mean more to me than you can ever imagine, so thank you for it. From the bottom of my heart, thank you.

Yours Sincerely
Jay Bhatti

Prologue

No matter how long he stared at the face on his mobile, he couldn't help but wonder why his old friend needed this prick of a politician dead so soon. The regular jobs he'd done for him in the past were never this extreme, nothing beyond scaring some politicians or government officials into following his direction. There were a couple of brutal beatings on individuals who were causing him grief, an odd job once when he needed him to steal sensitive files; however, murdering someone was a strange thing for him to ask. Still, he didn't take it to heart.

He didn't care why his friend needed him dead so soon. It's something he never gave much thought to when his clients required the use of his unique talents. His only concern was the hefty payment he would collect afterwards for another successful kill.

He tossed the mobile on top of his battered holdall bag as he glanced towards his driver. He still considered him a tad too young to assist with his job but had little choice of candidates at such short notice. On these rare occasions when he needed support with a particular contract, he would analyse every aspect of their service history to determine if they were a suitable match. However, he couldn't be picky with a deadline of only a day to complete the job. He, therefore, had no choice but to choose from the handful of applicants he considered competent. Still, the driver was doing a decent job so far. Throughout their journey down the M1, he didn't cause any significant accidents. He also hadn't pissed off any nearby drivers who'd remember his face if they raced past to give him the finger.

The only issue he had to contend with was his persistent need to start a conversation. For that reason, he sat in the back to avoid trying to spark another pointless discussion. He didn't mind small talk, just not on the job. There were still too many variables to consider as he devised his strategy. He didn't have time to waste in pointless debates whining about some bullshit red card ruling, the hottest TV shows he needed to catch up on, or the warmer spring days we've been experiencing. After finishing the job, he'd share a beer with him and discuss whatever mindless crap he wanted. That was, of course, if he didn't screw up. If he did, it would just be a bullet in the head. It's nothing personal, just the way life is in this job.

He glanced at the sat-nav after they merged into the M6. A hundred thirty miles from now, they would arrive in Liverpool. After that, it would take another twenty miles until they were outside the target's location. He estimated they'd reach the city within two hours, with no significant collisions or slow drivers clogging up the lanes from the evening rush hour.

So he sat back, formulating his strategy to eliminate the first of his latest victims.

Chapter 1

Almost every day of the week, hundreds if not thousands of people across the globe will spend their night in a hotel. It could be for an erotic weekend away with the partner, an urgent, much-deserved family break with the kids, or just a place to crash when you're travelling the world. All of them will pass through the doors of a hotel at one point or another.

It was no different for the Star Hotel. Over the past few days, as part of their plan to bring in a new high-class clientele, they had to house scores of party members who made the trip down to Liverpool to make a big splashy show on the latest eco-friendly initiative. It was a means for them to seem more likeable to the public by helping preserve our planet from ecological extinction. It's come about from all the growth rates of pollution we still need to face, thanks to corporations who refuse to adapt to the changing world.

Dressed in their finest clothes, smiling from ear to ear, they ventured out to meet the public, shaking every single hand they could. This way, come election time next year, their vote would 100% belong to their party instead of the opposition. Each member recognises, they have no protection without a favourable majority in parliament. All it took was one off-colour scandal, an inappropriate comment to the media, or not supporting the right policies, and bam! With just a quick snap of the fingers, you're out. Your seat in parliament is no more, along with all the perks that come with it. Stuck on the backbench, if lucky, and forced to wait years before regaining any power back. Then, by that point, you're unable to do anything meaningful, making your entire career seem like a waste of time.

Still, after four long, demanding days, the convention had finally reached its desired conclusion. The MPs and their teams shared a general sense of optimism, believing they had shown enough face to be remembered when the time came. However, for the staff of the Star Hotel, it was a completely different scenario. None of them cared if anyone had done well or not. Their only concern was for things to return to a sense of normality.

The staff were ill-prepared to deal with these high-end events, especially anything on this scale, where the ferocity of the event had left the team quite battered. Still, they just needed to survive one last night; then, it would officially be over, and the attendees would finally go home. Thanks to a stroke of luck, though, most of them had retreated to their rooms for an earlier night. The intensity of the last few days had left them depleted. All they wanted was to climb into bed and sleep till morning without being disturbed. Those who had yet to call it a night retreated to the lobby bar to celebrate their apparent success. They downed drink after drink, laughing the night away. It was the only time they'd had to relax since arriving, and they wanted to enjoy it ahead of returning to the capital.

Seeing them all indulge in life drove Laura envious as she sat alone, watching them from her receptionist's desk. Like the rest of her colleagues, she felt exhausted after working multiple double shifts to support the hotel; still, she kept it to herself. She was still a newcomer to the position, starting less than nine weeks ago. She was keen to maintain her favourable impression on the bosses during her final few weeks of probation by not complaining. No matter how much she wished, she could.

Like everyone else, the hotel crammed her days with errands after errands from the guests. It included everything from organising additional rooms, ensuring their clothes got washed, pressed and ironed for the morning, and copying and binding mountains of their paperwork every hour, on the hour. Their to-do list grew longer with each passing day; still, Laura kept at it with a smile, never losing her poise. After all, the guests' happiness is the most important thing for the hotel. No matter how cruel or unfriendly they were, and they were, Laura represented the Star Hotel. Their reputation was far more valuable than her feelings or those of her colleagues. The reputation drove the bookings, powered the lights, and kept everyone with a steady paycheck for their mortgages. If any guests were too badmouth the hotel and trash it online for its rude, unappreciative staff, it would destroy them. It would murder their bookings and profit margins, leaving them all as just another statistic for the unemployment list.

The evening, however, felt like it would be the exact opposite, with all the pressures of the last few days fading away as if they had never existed. Laura just sat at her desk, scrolling through a few websites on her computer, unaware of anything around her.

"Hello there, I would like to check in," said a soft voice.

It startled Laura, who was too busy fixed at her screen, to have noticed the gentleman who'd approached her desk. She shot up like a spring hare, remembering her training, as she straightened herself to greet him. He was a scruffy individual, older than he seemed, only carrying some battered holdall bag across his back. At first, it took her a moment to notice it, being too fixated on the innocent, charming demeanour slapped across his face.

A warm smile spread across Laura's face as she tried to appear more welcoming to the gentleman.

"Apologies, sir. I'm afraid I didn't see you come in."

The gentleman chuckled to himself as he returned the smile.

"Oh please, it's all good. You don't need to worry about it."

Laura felt a wee bit smitten by him. She couldn't blame herself, especially over the last few days, with the convention's attendees not being the friendliest in the world. This was mainly due to their snarky comments, screaming at her for what were genuine mistakes. None of them gave a damn she was on her own, still learning. Despite this, they still expected her to handle dozens, if not hundreds, of their tasks at once without failing a single one. So, for Laura to hear someone speak with such kindness, who clearly understood that mistakes are a part of human nature, was a much-needed change of pace.

"I appreciate it, sir. Thank you."

"It's my pleasure. Anyone in your line of work already has to deal with a lot of nonsense. There's no need for me to add it when you've done nothing wrong."

"You're too kind for this world, sir."

"Now that's something I've never been accused of," he quipped.

"Well, you are, at least to me." Laura lost herself as she daydreamed about the handsome stranger beside her for a moment. Her mind wandered to a life they could share and build before she snapped back to reality. She remembered her work that she was still on probation and had a job to do.

"I'm sorry, sir, but may I ask what your name is? For the booking, that is."

"Oh, of course, it's Smith. John Smith," he said, fixing his sights on her.

Laura shifted her gaze to the screen, entering his name into the system.

"Ah, yes, our last-minute bookie, I wondered if you were still planning to show up or not," she said, turning around to fetch the key card with John's eyes, watching her every move.

"The traffic up here was a nightmare. As usual, an accident on the M6 took quite a while to clear, hence why I'm so late."

"No worries, sir. The good news is we still made your room up for you, so you'll have no issues here." She placed the key card in front of him. "Do you have anything interesting planned for your stay?"

"I'm just down here for a bit of a school reunion. However, I misread my calendar, thinking it was next Wednesday instead of today, hence the last-minute booking. I'm just planning to drop off my bag and freshen up a bit before meeting them."

Laura grinned, knowing his predicament all too well. "Don't worry, sir, I've been mucking dates up like that since I can remember. The main thing is you're here right now, and that's all that matters."

"Cheers," John nodded, peering around at the growing commotion in the bar behind him before he re-locked eyes with Laura. He then placed his elbows on her desk with friendly gestures towards her. It caused a slight quiver to race down her spine, thinking her single stint was about to end. Sure, there was an age difference between them, with him being closer to his forties than she was, still in her twenties, but it didn't matter. Age is just a number. All she ever wanted was a guy who'd treat her with respect and be there for her without wanting something for themselves. It was a trait that she wished she could find in more people. Still, as he leaned in closer, she felt she might find it with him if he were to ask right now.

"Can I ask what's with all the suits in the bar behind us?"

Laura froze at his question, thinking it was the last place the conversation was heading. Still, she concealed her disappointment behind her smile, not letting it affect her persona. It's a lesson she had learned all her life about how to deal with rejections such as these.

"Oh, those people were just here for the convention that ended today," she said as if nothing had changed.

John glanced around at the bar, scanning the crowd as they sipped their drinks.

"Hmm, interesting. What kind of convention is, or was it?" He asked, more intrigued by the second, as he turned to face Laura.

"It's some government thing. I'm afraid I don't know the ins or outs."

"That's fine, thanks. I was just curious, but can I ask, just between us, of course? What are these government people like to be around?"

Laura did a quick check to see if anyone nearby might overhear them. Luckily, there were no staff or guests around who might tell her off or think she was a disloyal employee for blabbing, so she leaned in towards him.

"Between us, in the few days I've been serving them, they're easily the most demanding people I've ever had to deal with," she said with a slight giggle.

John shot her a cheeky grin, leaning in closer until they almost touched. "I can only imagine, but, let me guess, they're quite a demanding bunch of pricks, with all sorts of ridiculous demands?"

His answer delighted her. It didn't matter that their conservation wasn't shifting back towards them, even though she wished it would. Instead, Laura just felt gladder to have finally found someone with whom she could vent about these people without sounding like a disgruntled employee, looking to piss over the people who gave her a job when others wouldn't.

"Believe me. I've been running around like a dog, doing errands for them without even so much as a thank you or a simple please. It's even worse since they've taken the whole eighth floor to themselves, so I've got to keep darting upstairs every few minutes to pass their messages on, as they refuse to come down for them, the lazy bastards."

"It doesn't sound that terrible to me," he replied, confident she'd keep at it.

"It is. — Trust me on that, still, to top everything off, they have some six-foot guard checking me over every time I walk into one of the rooms like I'm some threat."

Laura gasped for breath, realising she hadn't spoken so candidly in such a long time.

John chuckled in response, keeping her entertained as his smile turned into a massive, stupid grin.

"What?—Seriously? Is our prick of a prime minister upstairs or something? As that is someone I'd love to have a few choice words with about what's best for this nation."

"I am glad to say it's a big fat no. I'd rather quit than serve that buffoon under any circumstances."

"I'd be so proud of you if you did that. So, who is it then?"

"It's a secretary, advisor type of person. I'm not sure exactly what he does, but everyone keeps reminding me he's important. Either way, I have to do my part to stay in his good graces. As instructed by the hotel, of course," she said, masking the growing blush in her cheeks as best she could.

Once the words hit John's eardrums, he just chuckled to himself, like Laura had told a joke that only he could understand. He then swiped the key card from the counter and placed it in his pocket without glancing at it.

"Well, thank you very much for the chat, but I'd best be heading off. I wouldn't want to be any later than I already am."

Laura realised nothing was likely to happen between them as she wanted; still, she didn't care in the end. She was just thankful for the interaction she'd shared with this handsome stranger, no matter how brief it lasted. It was, without a doubt, the most joyous moment in the entire convention for her and something she wouldn't soon forget.

"All the best, Mr Smith, and thank you for the talk too," she added, still hopeful he would give her his number to see if this would lead anywhere.

John, however, just nodded back, stepping away in silence, as he crossed the lobby towards the elevator. Then, along with his smile, he finally dropped his facade.

Chapter 2

John reached the elevator, pressed the controls, and waited for it to arrive. He scrutinised every face in the lobby for a potential threat, but it was all clear. The only people around were those already in the bar, drinking away, unaware of his presence. Only the receptionist glimpsed in his direction. He had the sense she wanted him to come back and sweep her off her feet like in all those sappy romcoms he figured she watched on repeat. Still, John had zero intention of doing anything with her. He'd already got what he was after. He, however, still smiled at her as he stepped into the elevator, clicking the keypad to keep his appearance up. Then, once the doors closed and started moving, John lost his smile.

He straightened himself up, extending his neck out, pushing his shoulder blades together like he was stretching out before a big workout. After a couple of rotations, John adjusted his bag to hang by his side instead of his back, making it easier to reach for as he unzipped it. He was ready for action as the elevator opened.

The floor was silent as John stepped on it. As he glanced across both sides of the hallway, he spotted a lone individual standing next to one of the corner rooms. His suit was grey and straightforward, nothing special, but it gave him a sense of professionalism. He wore it with a serious, *'I'm working'* expression on his face. Combined with his posture and trademark military buzzcut, he appeared pretty intimidating for a man of his build. Still, none of it prevented John from walking straight up to him with a broad, stupid grin slapped across his face.

The man's manner became quite stern once John approached him. "Can I help you, sir?" he asked with a grim expression, except John didn't seem at all fazed. He instead stood with glee, like he was meeting his childhood hero.

"I know this may be inappropriate to ask, but you are a bodyguard, aren't you?"

His question threw the bodyguard as he stood, subtly scanning the stranger, trying to figure out who he was. However, he couldn't determine anything from his appearance except that he looked like a hipster without a beard. Nothing seemed out of place, and, in all fairness, he seemed pretty normal, aside from his overactive behaviour. Still, he remained firm when he replied.

"How does it concern you, sir?"

"If you are, I've always wanted to know: what's it honestly like to protect another human being?" he asked in awe as if he were clamouring for a celebrity's autograph.

The bodyguard just stared, bemused, taken aback by the weirdness of his question and, in fact, the entire situation. He never had to deal with anything like this during all his years of service. It's a unique situation they don't train you for, people shooting and trying to kill you in a hazardous environment that he knew how to handle easily; he'd done it half his life. However, there's no natural response for some stranger trying to make chitchat about the pleasures of personal protection. He was entirely out of his element as he contemplated what to say.

After a few seconds of further scrutiny, detecting no sign of hostility, the bodyguard realised the most effective way forward was to indulge the strange individual by answering his questions, if only to help him understand what he was after.

"It's a fine job, though I'm not sure what you want me to say about it," he admitted, wondering if that was a good enough reply or not.

John, however, kept smiling like he didn't have a care in the world.

"No worries. It was just a question I always dreamed of asking if I ever had the chance to meet someone like yourself up close in person, and now I have."

The bodyguard stood there, astonished by the strangeness of what just transpired. His confusion only increased by the second, as both men shot each other awkward glances without uttering a word. The stranger wasn't moving away. He instead seemed to be waiting for something to happen as his gaze shifted around the hallway; however, it was the least of his concerns. If his employer emerged right now, it would appear he was slacking on the job. He knew it wouldn't be a pretty look for him, especially after his previous warnings regarding his worsening conduct. So, he raised his arms out to guide the stranger away.

"Alright, sir, if you would care to continue with your eve—," but John cut him off mid-sentence.

"Can I ask who you're protecting right now? Someone famous?" he inquired, looking around the hallway, that to his delight, still contained only the two of them.

"No, that's not possible," the bodyguard remarked, unaware of the peril ahead once he nudged the stranger away.

John's entire persona switched like the toss of a coin as he fixed eyes on him. Then, finally, he abandoned his pretence to ask: "James Baker is in the room behind you, isn't he?"

The bodyguard froze in his tracks once he grasped what the stranger had said. After that, his entire mind grew manic. It was awash with a tsunami of questions and thoughts. He attempted to speak some of them but couldn't put the words together due to them constantly tripping over in his mouth.

How does he know that? Wait, is this a test of some sort? Have I done a decent job, or will they fire me for talking? Christ, I can't afford to be unemployed right now, not with my mortgage. Oh, hell, my wife will murder me over this mess if she doesn't just leave m— Hold on, wait, no, wait — is this an actual threat?

Except none of it mattered.

John saw the reaction on his face and smiled. He knew he had just verified the identity of his target, so he responded in kind to his generosity by clenching his fist and striking him in the gut.

The bodyguard lost his balance, stumbling onto the ground from the blow. John continued his assault, snatching the bodyguard by the head and ramming him against the wall behind. After forcing him to stand, John twisted him around, slamming him face-first into the wall beside him before striking him in the back of the thigh bone. It caused the bodyguard to tumble down once again.

In quick succession, John yanked a Glock Seventeen with a silencer attached from his bag, pressing it against the base of the bodyguard's skull.

"Quietly up you come," John whispered into his ear.

The bodyguard, unbalanced and confused, followed his instructions to the letter, standing up as best he could despite the stabbing pain. John glanced around the hallway for one last time, and as he predicted, it was silent. Anybody who wasn't in the bar downstairs or within earshot of this area had heard nothing. It meant he was free to knock on his targets' doors without interference.

He didn't have to wait long. Within seconds, the door swung open as an annoyed gentleman stepped out. He was ready to unleash an angry tirade against the person responsible for interrupting his night. However, all those words faded when he saw the bodyguard sworn to protect him, bleeding with uncontrollable fear in his eyes. He instead stood motionless, whiter than he had ever been in his life, unable to concentrate.

His limbs were trembling at the sight of the stranger with the gun.

John knew he wasn't the target, having studied him all evening. Still, not wanting the gentleman to do anything foolish, he raised his Glock and squeezed the trigger back. In a mere millisecond, a single bullet entered the chamber, passing straight through the barrel into the skull of the unknown man.

Once his lifeless body collapsed to the floor, John swiftly rammed his pistol back against the bodyguard's head, forcing him inside before his reflexes could kick in. After the door clicked shut with both of them inside, John shot the bodyguard through the base of his skull, tossing him on the floor like he was nothing. Blood trickled out of his latest victim's heads as John repositioned himself, creeping into the room.

It only took six steps before he found James Baker, his intended target. Baker sat on the bed, petrified over what was happening, still clutching the papers he seemed to have been studying. John fixed the barrel in his face while he scanned the rest of the room. He searched for anyone he might have missed prior to focusing his full attention on his target.

"I take it there's no one else in the room," he remarked.

Baker staggered as he glanced behind, spotting the blood splatters on the wall from his friend.

"It was only him," he said with a whimper before facing the barrel aimed at his face. Then, finally, he straightened himself out, finding some level of vigour, and said, "Do you have any idea who I am? I'm the home secretary, for Christ's sake."

But, it was futile. John just smiled, trying not to laugh at his pitiful excuse for a threat.

"Like I give a shit, you idiot," he said, clicking the trigger, shooting the secretary like the others with a single bullet through the forehead. It was his signature style. The secretary's body slumped over the bedsheets, soaking them in his blood, like the carpet his friends laid on.

Without a second's hesitation, John readjusted himself. He aimed the pistol at the door, listening to all the noises outside the room. Thirty seconds ticked by, and nothing happened. It was silent. The same thing occurred after another thirty. There were no screams of terror, alarms buzzing in the eardrum, or footsteps of eavesdroppers rushing away for their lives. He was clear. No one was aware of the tragedy that had just taken place inside this room.

John's smile grew as he tucked his Glock away and dumped his holdall in a cupboard, having no use for it now. He then checked himself over for any signs of bloodstains. Then, after ensuring he was clean, John left the scene with care, avoiding any fresh blood splatters settling into the carpet. Outside, he flipped the do not disturb sign over, strolling over to the elevator without a care for who he'd murdered.

John pressed the button, and within ninety-three seconds, he was back in the lobby. He spotted the receptionist, who was busy helping a guest with some queries. John made sure not to draw her eye while he exited the hotel. He then kept at a steady pace as he worked his way into the car park, where he locked eyes with a second-hand BMW. John walked over to it, checking over his shoulder every few seconds, an unconscious habit he'd cultivated since Iraq to guarantee no one would get the drop on him. Once he was sure nobody was watching, he slid into the back of the vehicle.

It startled the young individual sitting in the driver's seat who, despite having combat experience, failed to notice someone sneaking up behind him. The driver twisted around, clenching his fist for a fight, but once he saw it was his boss, he eased his grip, sighing with relief. Still, he kept staring, waiting for an answer to a question he didn't have the nerve to ask.

John, however, remained focused, scanning the car park for threats until he realised they were still stationary and turned to his driver.

"Matthew, what are you waiting for? Secretary's dead, let's go," he barked.

His response didn't faze him. On the contrary, Matthew was thrilled to hear the answer he'd been hoping for.

"North, that's spectacular work. It truly is," he said, starting the engine and driving off as he left the hotel in his rearview mirror.

Free of his facade, North sat back, pondering if that needy receptionist would be the one to find the bodies come morning. He couldn't help but think it would be the ultimate middle finger for all the shit she had to deal with. It was a horrific notion North couldn't help but crack up about.

Chapter 3

The sun rose over a brand-new day in the capital as residents awoke to a new dawn. Another wonderful spring day lay ahead, despite everyone knowing you can't rely on the English weather to stay consistent. Most of its residents were still in a haze from their dreams when they awoke, wishing they could stay in bed for an extra few minutes. Still, this wasn't the case for the latest member of the Section, Naomi Ripley.

She was already deep into her early morning run, spiriting across an empty city at a breakneck speed, leaping down stairwells, sliding over cars, darting through traffic. Then, with a rush of adrenaline, she hurtled herself through the city centre at lightning speed, an all-time high far superior to her previous runs, as she pushed whatever muscles she had that bit more. It didn't even matter that her laces were coming undone; she just pressed on, not wanting to lose her momentum. It was in stark contrast to the rest of the population, who had just rolled out of bed to switch their alarms off for the second time since tapping the snooze button.

Ripley sprinted across Millennium Bridge, stopping in the middle to catch her breath, having exerted her body to the limit but smiling. As her speed increased, she knew she was making progress. After all, it was always about seconds for her in her line of work. The faster she was, the greater her chances were of preventing the atrocities she faced from happening.

She stood on the edge of the bridge, watching the sunrise's reflection across the river in complete awe. Agency life had left her no time to enjoy the simple things, so she seized the chance to appreciate the beauty of such a sight. It looked like a riot of colours. The sun refracted across the river, giving the water its trademark golden tint. It was a true sight to behold and one she was glad to have finally seen. She leaned across the edge, recalling her training. She took shorter and shorter breaths to lower her heart rate, allowing her muscles to heal from the workout.

As she recovered, Ripley gazed around at the city she had vowed to defend, her home appreciating the elegance in its design. It had a warm blue hue that shone over it. The air was heavy with the stench of a city in constant flux, alive with the dreams of its people.

She'd never visited the capital during her twenty-five years of life. She was a stranger to this site, having lived the bulk of her childhood in various other nations because of her father's constant re-deployment. His talents as a commander made him a sought-after soldier in times of conflict for the UK. He was a man who was always willing to assist whatever the situation required while never losing sight of his role as a father. He always took Ripley with him wherever he lived, despite how hostile the places seemed. He never wanted to be without her, knowing she was safer with him than anywhere else. The frequent changes in her upbringing allowed Ripley to attain a broader appreciation and knowledge of cultures and the world than most kids her age. This was true no matter what school she attended. It was these traits that made her the ideal recruit for the Section, an attribute further validated by her bravery on the Balkans frontier.

NATO deployed troops into the region to help stabilise it after a mass resurgence of ethnic cleansing. Fresh out of training, Ripley was a part of the first waves of countless units to enter the brawling chaos. It left masses of brave soldiers petrified of the bloodshed to come. Their fear stemmed from the sheer number of bullets that filled the air and the endless explosions that decimated the environments they trekked through. As they inhaled the never-ending scent of the dead, they were too late to save. The stench alone was enough to turn any obedient soldiers away. Still, Ripley refused to give in and pressed on. She was a fighter and always faced the enemy head-on, whatever the odds may have been if it meant preventing the deaths of her comrades. The courage she displayed brought her fellow soldiers to shame. As a result, many of them fled in terror. Still, those who remained firm continued to stand with Ripley, month after month, to end the horrific acts of atrocity they witnessed.

Throughout the campaign, Ripley proved to be a vital soldier in the field. She was willing to sacrifice all she was for anyone who would dare stand by her in such destructive affairs. This attitude towards life drew her to the Section. She'd heard the stories of their achievements, the lives they had saved, and wanted to be part of it. She wanted to stand against those who sought to diminish the things we cherished, just like her father before her.

It might have only been a few months since she left the army to join; still, in that time, Ripley had become one of their most promising agents to date. She dealt with everything from assassination attempts against foreign diplomats to dismantling local terrorist cells. Her most recent success came three weeks ago when she foiled an attack on a Sikh temple of worship.

She discovered from one of her sources that he helped smuggle some strange materials into an abandoned office block on the outskirts of Slough. Ripley headed into the block to investigate, as she did with all leads. It turned out that a militant radical had turned one of its floors into a makeshift bomb factory. It belonged to a man called Dragoslav. He was a disgraced relic of a bomb maker from the old ethnic cleansing days. For the past four years, Interpol had been hunting for him after bombings of holy temples across Western Europe, as a part of his one-man crusade against any ideology that wasn't the Christian faith. It was a belief he held in firm agreement with himself as he tried to garner more support for his cause through his attacks.

Not wanting him to escape or possibly trigger his attack while she waited for reinforcements to arrive as per protocol, Ripley stormed his hideout on her own. The sheer surprise of her move caught Dragoslav unprepared as she tackled him, shattering his femur as she pinned him against the ground. He attempted to wrestle her off but didn't have the resolve he once possessed in his youth.

In those days, he'd been able to swat off any women like her, as easy as crushing spiders. Still, it wasn't the same person Ripley kept nailed to the ground. He was nothing more than a frail elderly man now, overcome with hatred towards the woman who shattered his leg. Still, Dragoslav stared back, trying everything to hide the agony he felt. He tried to remain firm, just as he had learned all those years ago, like the loyalist to his cause he was.

Unfortunately, it did him no good. Ripley saw the fear he tried to mask and knew it wouldn't take much to remove. She struck him across his chin, keeping him awake as she thrashed down on his fractured leg, battering his nerves with hit after hit. She didn't stop, even though she noticed tears running down his cheek. Instead, she just continued. He was a murderer, nothing more. Ripley didn't see any reason to show restraint, not with the bodies he'd left behind.

Dragoslav did all he could to withstand the pain she poured into him from each strike. However, in his current state, with his fraying age, he couldn't hold his nerve for long and so eventually surrendered to her.

The information he revealed allowed the Section to prevent the compound explosive he built from being used against hundreds of innocent worshippers whose chosen faith didn't merit such a heinous end.

The act and her other accomplishments earned Ripley respect and admiration that others took an entire forty-plus-year career to achieve. It was a comfort for her to know that the people she worked with regarded her as someone they could depend on in times of need. She was proud to wear it as it gave her the confidence to do what she did every day.

Ripley's brief appreciation of the city didn't last long once her mobile buzzed away in her pocket. It didn't faze her. Out-of-hour calls were a natural part of agency life, given how an attack could occur at any second. It doesn't matter what time of day it is; they would need her ready and able to step in without thinking twice. So, like a muscle reflex, Ripley whipped out her mobile.

"What's the story today, Harper?"

As the voice on the other end explained the news to her, Ripley straightened herself up, realising the type of threat she was about to face.

"Copy that. I'm on my way in."

Ripley ended the call, fastening her lace before bolting across the bridge, preparing herself to face her newest threat.

Chapter 4

The operations hub the Section operates out of every day of the week is about the size of any typical office space. Still, for the agents who worked for them, it was just how they liked it. The fundamental purpose of the Section was to deal with all high-profile attacks on British soil. They have seen everything from political assassinations on state visits to chemical attacks in street markets and every horrendous act in between. It could be from extremists wanting revenge for something that happened tens of thousands of miles away, foreign powers looking to advance their control, or lone assailants wishing to settle scores. The Section was who the government turned to prevent them from occurring. No matter what type of threat it was, they would always stand their ground.

It's why agents that work for them are such a tight-knit group of individuals. In the seventeen years since the unit's establishment, they have prevented countless attacks and catastrophes, from this one room. The fundamental reason for that was that everyone who worked, or works, for the Section trusted one another without question. It didn't matter whether they sat behind a desk or out in the field; each agent faced the same horrors side by side. It's the only way they could stop the carnage that sociopaths and extremists in the world want to inflict on their home.

This meant trusting those around them to do their jobs without fault and, frankly, going beyond what any human can rightfully expect or ask of themselves. It was their burden to ensure the public they swore to protect was never in harm's way, even if it meant sacrificing their own life. It's a notion they all must learn to live with, that despite every individual's skill and trust in one another, not all agents will make it out alive. As a result, the unit has been through scores of personal changes since its foundation. Some agents die in the field. Others leave because of their inability to cope with the pressures of this life. Meanwhile, others transferred out to other departments because they were unfit for the role or the Section. This was no different from Ripley's predecessor.

He'd sustained significant injuries in trying to capture a known terrorist. The agent chased the target into an industrial yard, thinking he had the upper hand. However, he was impulsive, disregarding orders to wait for support, too fixated on capturing his prize to see it was a ruse. Then, as he entered the yard, it happened. His target's friends were hiding in the shadows for him, and once he got close, they ambushed him with a hail of gunfire. Luckily, the Section had monitored his movements, so they got paramedics to him within minutes of the first bullet ripping into his flesh. Then, after thirteen hours of gruelling surgical procedures, he was alive, except never the same again after removing bullet after bullet. He'd lost all his motor function and the ability to do anything for himself. It meant that he lived out the rest of his life with a team of nurses checking in on him four times a day, fearing that he would defecate himself in their absence. It left him as nothing more than a cold reminder of the daily cost this lifestyle presents.

Still, in spite of all the frequent losses, the one thing that remained consistent was the trusted eye of Alife Harper. He was an individual who had dedicated the better part of his thirty-year career to working as the Section's communication chief. It was a blessing to have him in his prime, even now. No one in the whole of the British service was better suited to run surveillance than him. He might not be as young as his co-workers, but the skills he'd developed throughout his celebrated career were as sharp as ever. His attention to detail, fused with his ability to process information at lightning speed, made him the ideal researcher to combat the threats that plagued them.

He was meticulous in his research, searching through bottomless pits of surveillance footage. His eyes would scrutinise every square frame, hunting for any clue that would lead the Section to the individual responsible for the atrocities they faced. Still, no matter how tedious or draining the task seemed, Harper took it in his stride. He knew that the constant checks he prided himself on allowed the Section to remain one step ahead of their enemies and one step closer to stopping them.

As always, Harper sat alone at his desk, concentrating on his work, meaning he never noticed when Ripley or anyone else approached him. She'd switched from her running gear to a pair of trousers with a sweatshirt, boots, and jacket on top.

She waved a cup of coffee that she was holding in front of him. "Black with three sugars. Figured you would need the extra kick today."

Harper gazed up with glee, grabbing hold of the drink.

"You're a lifesaver," he said, taking a sip.

"Don't sweat it."

He leaned back in his chair, turning towards her, looking more relaxed than he'd been. "So, how far did you make it in your run today before my call?"

Ripley smirked, leaning up against the edge of his desk. "Halfway through this time, I keep hoping there won't be a threat until the afternoon one of these days, so I can actually finish a run."

"One can only dream, my dear."

Harper perked up as the caffeine kicked in. "So, how is it coming along, anyway? Do you feel any faster?"

"A little. I'm on the right track. I only need more time to build on what I have."

"If you need some time, I recommend not coming in on your days off. It could do wonders for your body."

"You know, I could say the same about you. Doesn't your wife miss having you around at all?"

"She suffers from it sometimes, like everyone's better halves in this place. Still, our secret to making sure it doesn't hurt as much as it can is we always ensure to have our dinner, or failing that, our breakfast together. No phones, devices or any other rubbish, just us. That way, we can spend some real-time together instead of none at all."

"That's sweet, Alife."

Harper nodded in agreement. "It served us well for nearly a quarter-century and hopefully for many more years ahead, so consider giving it a whirl sometime. Instead of, you know, spending all your free time running, try and find someone."

"Yeah, when the country isn't under threat, I'll give it a shot, see if I can find that ideal breakfast partner."

"Hey, don't knock it. You deserve to have someone. I mean, whatever happened to the girl from accounting you were seeing? She seemed nice."

"I wouldn't call it seeing each other. It was just a couple of drinks at the pub after work, nothing more than that."

"Ah, what a shame. You two could have made such a lovely couple."

As he said this, Ripley couldn't help but smile. "Yeah, she's a sweet girl and all, but I couldn't picture us going any further after hearing how much mindless crap she could spew out on repeat."

"Still, what could've been? Let's just pray that there are no awkward issues if you run into each other now."

"Nah, it will be fine. We ended it on good terms. Besides, I'm pretty sure she wasn't warming up to me anyway, so we both kind of dodged a bullet there. Still, I am on the lookout for Ms Right; as they say, I am, and who knows, maybe one day I'll be lucky enough to have what you have."

"Well, let's just hope that day isn't too far off for you," Harper said, raising his cup. He then downed the last of his coffee in one big gulp before throwing it away. Ripley stared at him, surprised by the speed he'd finished it.

"I'm sorry, but did you leave this place last night? And you know, see that wife of yours," she teased.

"I did nosey, but like the idiot I am, I volunteered to come in early to help cover the overnight shift. They're still down one person, with Maria in Sweden after her mother's stroke. I figured it would give me time to catch up on some backlog reports, but I was mistaken. Once the call came in about the home secretary, Denver declared everything was on hold until we locate his killer."

"Yeah, I read his bullet points on the way down. No doubt this is a pro we're dealing with. I mean, no ordinary citizen would have the balls to walk into a public hotel and gun down the home secretary, no matter how much they hated his guts. I know it's early, but are there any leads?"

"Nothing yet, I'm afraid. However, I got my facial algorithm running on everyone in the hotel last night via their CCTV footage. No hits yet, but it's only been running for a few minutes. Still, we may know more when Denver comes in."

"Speaking of, where is our commander-in-chief?"

"Briefing with the PM," Harper said, peeking behind her as he noticed someone walking in. "Speaking of the devil, here he is."

Ripley turned around, seeing her boss, Elliot Denver, strolling in. He was an ageing man in his late-fifties with his hair greying in the back and a face covered in age spots and wrinkles. It's a direct by-product of working in British intelligence for nearly three-quarters of your life. Still, despite his appearance, Denver was as sharp as ever. It's why he has stuck around so long, managing the Section since its inception. It was his one and only offspring he'd spent the last seventeen years shaping to his liking.

The truth is, though, the Section doesn't and will never work without him. He's led every version of his team through each crisis, fallen agent, and every one of its successes. He's a man who never failed to ensure the right people paid for the crimes of attacking his country, regardless of who they may be. As in Denver's simplistic view of life, everyone is accountable for their crimes. No back-end agreements, political sway, threats of reprisals from foreign powers, or zealot terrorist cells would prevent him from implementing true justice. It was something he was prouder of than any of the medals he had received. The Section was his life, and when someone dared to attack the country he'd called home, there was no stopping him.

Denver approached them straight on with a stiff stance. Ripley pushed off the desk, standing tall, while Harper straightened himself up, readjusting his tie. Denver was a stickler for appearances, given his extensive career in the military, combined with his upbringing in boarding schools. It drove him to believe that everyone should look their best at all times, a courtesy he extended to his team.

"I take it we don't have any leads yet," he stated.

Harper peeked at his screen, double-checking his work before addressing him. "I'm afraid not, but my algorithm is still running."

Denver shook his head in disappointment but didn't let it phase him. "Hopefully, that will shed light on what happened last night. The PM informed me he wants this resolved as soon as possible. With the upcoming election, he's worried the secretary's death will weaken his party and jeopardise his re-election chances, so as you can guess, he isn't happy about any of this."

"Did the PM give you anything to act on?" Ripley asked.

"No, nothing that will help us, but according to the whispers I've heard, there are individuals glad he's dead. It's no secret that the home secretary pissed off many people in his career, apart from us. Regardless, though, we need to move fast. This news becomes public within the hour, and when that happens, the press will hound them for answers and for us to find his killer."

Soon after, a ping sounded from Harper's screen, followed by a face popping up showing last night's receptionist chatting to a gentleman. The algorithm had found its match.

Harper leapt to his keyboard, hitting various commands to bring up all the details of the individual, smiling. However, once he saw who it was, his smile vanished.

"We have a match, sir, but it's far from good news," he announced.

Denver and Ripley hovered over Harper's screen, inspecting who this mystery person was.

"David North," Denver remarked with despair, knowing his face only too well.

Ripley stared at the screen, disgusted by the man. She was well aware of who he was and what his presence meant for the type of threat they now faced.

"Time-wise, he arrives around the hour we estimate the secretary died. So, when you add that to his well-known reputation, there's no doubt it's him, sir," Harper noted.

Denver stood back, absorbing the information over the last few seconds, thinking it all over as he realised the danger this one man now posed to them. He pictured the carnage that would surely follow as they sought him out like before, the bodies he would leave behind.

"Of course, it's him. This was always his style, high-risk, high-profile targets, anything to feel that damn rush."

Denver couldn't help but lower his brow. He tried to contain the hatred he harboured for this one man before straightening himself and focusing his efforts on working the threat at hand.

"Harper, trace his movements from him entering the hotel to leaving it and everything in-between. No matter how irrelevant it may appear to you, I want it tracked."

Harper nodded in agreement. He knew that when Denver gave you an order, everything else you were doing had to be put to one side until you had carried it out. His fingers started typing away as he cycled through the hotel's footage, frame by frame, searching for North.

Denver, meanwhile, tapped Ripley on the shoulder. "A word in my office, if you don't mind," he said as Ripley accompanied him into his domain.

Chapter 5

Denver was a stickler for keeping things simplistic, not having much in terms of meaningful possessions. He'd never seen their appeal, having grown up without the latest *"it object,"* believing them more of a distraction than a functioning tool that can benefit life productively. He reflected on this in the style of his office, plain and unassuming. It contained only a single corner desk with an assortment of stationery spread across it, with a couple of chairs for guests. The only thing that stood out was a framed photo of Denver with his old army unit. It clashed with the rest of the layout because of its level of colour, but it didn't bother him. Instead, it was the only thing he cared about from his past to remember. After all, the army had made him into the man he is today.

He was a boy of twenty who rose through the ranks during the first Gulf war, serving, by choice, as an infantryman on the front line. For him, it was the ideal position to assist in his mission to help as many of his fellow soldiers survive the conflict that lay ahead. He had no intention of watching the friends who'd supported and stood by him in training when he wanted to give in, die in vain, as a part of a conflict his commanders didn't expect them to survive.

As depicted one late afternoon on a return journey to base, Denver's unit vehicle came under fire by a wave of enemy insurrectionists waiting in hiding for them. For weeks, they studied their patrols, following their routes, the places they travelled, and the time they spent in each one before moving on to the next. It was all about finding the ideal place to launch their attack before reinforcements arrived and overwhelmed them. Then, after weeks of searching, they found their dream position after learning that the soldiers provide food to a local village outside their base each week. As time wore on, they kept track of the town. Without fail, the unit would make the same trip every Sunday, bringing its residents as much food as possible. With their position secured, they set up their ambush and unleashed hell once they were on their way home the following week.

The surprise of the attack caught the men unprepared. Their vision became blurred by a constant flurry of bullets penetrating the vehicles. The impact tore the engines apart in no time as they came to an abrupt stop. At that moment, every member of that unit remained frozen, their bodies bleeding out from every bullet that hacked through the bodywork, cutting into their flesh.

There was nothing they could do but lie motionless, making peace with their gods for a merciful end. In the distance, they watched them approach, weapons at the ready, helpless to do anything but wait. Just wait as they close their eyes, preparing for their final few seconds. However, the moment they took aim, the men escaped death when Denver injured himself, hoisted his rifle, and stood his ground against a never-ending hail of bullets. He never faltered as he manifested his pain inside to keep the insurrectionists at bay, protecting those around him until support arrived to drive them off.

The heroism he exhibited that day didn't go unnoticed. His selfless efforts delighted the eyes of the intelligence agencies. They recognised he was a rare individual, a person of pure, noble character they wanted working in their midst.

Denver served with distinction in all the major conflicts within the Middle East in the late nineties and early-two-thousands, proving to be a vital rock during such vulnerable and unstable times. This trait convinced the head of MI5 that he was the right person to serve as the head of the newly established Section. Its sole purpose was to help defend the British mainland after the wars in the east found their way home. Seventeen years on, with the success of the Section and the catastrophes they thwarted, Denver had become one of British intelligence's most respected agents to date. He was someone they could always count on to protect their home once the latest crisis struck, that has yet again, come at the hands of David North.

The pair entered as Denver sat down at his desk, gesturing Ripley to take the chair in front.

"I take it you're aware of North's seeded history?" he inquired.

Ripley smirked at the comment as she sat down.

"Who isn't? He's the poster boy for agent gone native," she said without thinking.

Denver was however unimpressed with her remark as he stared back, wanting something more with substance from his lead field agent to know if she was ready.

After a moment of silence, Ripley knew what he wanted to hear.

"He's one of us, former intelligence hitman, precision high stakes killing, with a body count higher than most British soldiers, thanks to his extensive tours of Iraq. He also has a deeply unbiased mentality for not caring who he murders, which started long before he left the agency. Since then, well, we know who he's murdered out there, but that's North for you. Another unpassionate, relentless killer who'd grown tired of the orders given to him and so left to live his life as he pleased."

"You genuinely think that's the reason for him leaving?"

"Honestly, chief, I don't know. I don't think anyone knows what converted North or any of the countless predecessors before him into these types of murderers, who've lost the most basic aspects of decency and self-respect for the people they once belonged to in the first place?"

"True, very true," Denver muttered. It was a sentiment he understood all too well. For a long time, he encountered more than enough individuals like North to know there's never some definite answer for what shaped them into the people they are today: cruel, shameless murderers whose only loyalty lies to their bank accounts.

Denver laid in his chair, brushing his hand across the stubble on his face. He watched Ripley sit in front of him, knowing that after everything she'd accomplished in the Balkans, to her limited time here, she was ready. Despite the unimaginable danger this man posed, she was ready for it.

"Ripley, I'm sending you to Liverpool. If he hasn't disappeared, you're the best person to locate North. Nobody down there will be a match for someone like him, but I know you'll be able to handle yourself."

Ripley sat stunned as she let Denver's praise sink in.

"You honestly think I'm a match for North, sir?"

Her question didn't faze him. Denver had always seen more in his agents than they ever could. It was something he prided himself on by identifying the same honest traits someone once discovered in him. It lies in the willingness to elevate oneself above others for the sake of doing some good in this world. Unfortunately, it's a feature he found in short supply in this ever-changing world.

"You're the only person I trust who's capable of stopping him. He may have two decades of experience behind him, but you're as resourceful and skilled as he ever was. Maybe better."

Ripley sat in silence, pondering over what he had said, wondering if she was indeed the right person for the job. She'd been with the Section for a handful of months and done solid work, but this was something else altogether. North wasn't some misguided extremist who just wanted to cause widespread damage. Neither was he some undisciplined soldier ordered to fight and die for the glory of his nation's causes. Instead, he was a cold, calculated assassin with the same skill set she had, yet with a body count higher than anyone would care to admit. He'd spent years refining his natural killing ability to never falter on a single kill when asked. He never cared who they were – politicians, businessmen, diplomats, brothers, aunts, or daughters; whatever their age, it didn't matter. They were just the latest name on some file to him, nothing more.

Ripley felt unnerved, knowing the type of person Denver needed her to face, as he didn't shy away from his hatred of the man.

"But never underestimate North. Before he started this career of murdering for the highest bidder, he was an exceptional agent. He's spent a lifetime evading us, and he's back on British soil for the first time in years. It's our chance — our duty — to end his madness once and for all. However, let me clarify one thing: if you can bring him in alive, please do. North needs to serve true justice, paying for every death he's caused us, but, if that's not a viable option, I am ordering you to kill him."

Ripley didn't blink at his request. The stories of what North had done in the last few years had left a massive stain on the agency's name. There was no escaping from the fact they had trained and nurtured one of the most notorious contract killers on the planet. It didn't sit well with many foreign agencies, given North's growing reckless nature of walking into public areas and gunning his targets down. Even if it meant shooting through civilians, North wouldn't hesitate, not in the slightest. All that seemed to matter to him now was achieving the kill, no matter how many casualties he left in his wake. As for Denver, though, it was a more personal grievance since North murdered two of his agents in their last encounter.

After years of murdering from one nation to the next, the Section picked up North's trail, heading to Sudan on a supposed job. Denver tasked two agents with tracking him down and bringing him to justice. It wasn't something he usually did, sending agents overseas, but he was willing to make an exception for a chance to take down North. Unfortunately, while they were searching, North, unbeknownst to them, caught wind of their presence. He used it to his advantage, luring them into a trap by discreetly letting slip where he was hiding to the locals. Then, waiting in hiding outside, North mowed both of them down without a shred of mercy once they arrived to apprehend him, but he didn't stop there. As a further sign of disdain for their deaths, he used their mobiles to send a message to the Section, saying *"better luck next time,"* with an image of their bullet-ridden corpses.

Still, more than his grotesque joke, what stung Denver more was that they couldn't recover the bodies. The desert had buried them so deep that the families had to settle for a closed casket funeral. Since then, he's been waiting for a chance to avenge them, not just for his agents but for every single family member North had desecrated throughout his life.

They sat contemplating his deeds, the murderer he now was, when Harper entered the room.

Denver addressed him with anticipation but made sure it didn't alter his voice. "What did you find out?"

"I've tracked North leaving the hotel in a BMW 3 Series with an unknown assailant. It's unclear who. There's never a clean visual of their face for me to identify. However, the vehicle I could track ended up at a warehouse, about fourteen miles away, and according to all indications, it appears that it's still there.

Denver glanced at Ripley, who stared back, coming to the same dreaded conclusion. If North was indeed in London, murdering the home secretary was likely the start of something else; otherwise, he would have just vanished like usual.

"I'm not taking any chances with this. Until we find North, we must presume he's here to eliminate someone, most likely another government official, but there's never any telling, not with him."

Denver stroked the stubble across his chin as he lay in his chair, addressing Ripley. "Looks like you're staying here. Head down to that warehouse and find him. For all our sakes, find North."

Ripley stood without hesitation, ready for action, knowing how daunting the task was and the stakes involved. She, however, wasn't about to let Denver down, not with something as serious as this. His trust was unwavering and gave her all the confidence she needed to do the job.

"You have my word, chief. I'll stop whatever North has planned," Ripley said, nodding back to Denver in respect, as she turned towards Harper, leaving his office. "Message me the address and contact firearm support to have them meet me down there. I'm not messing around. I'm charging in hard and fast after him."

"Roger that. I'll keep you apprised of anything that happens on our end," Harper said as he turned towards his desk to make the call.

In the meantime, Ripley headed out on her mission to capture British intelligence's biggest disgrace to date, David North.

Chapter 6

Deep within an old disused loft unit, North laid up with his accomplice, preparing the next stage of his plan. They sat at separate tables across the room. Matthew was busy putting his weapon skills to work, with multiple pieces of disassembled Glocks in front of him. He meticulously removed all the dust particles clinging to each part with a tiny brush and cloth. The pistol malfunctioning is the one thing you never want happening when you squeeze the trigger. If that occurred in a shoot-out, you'd be dead within seconds. The most effective way to avoid it is to routinely strip down the firearm piece by piece and clean each section thoroughly. Matthew had it drilled into him throughout his training. The constant repetition made it one of the few things he was proficient at. He didn't mind it at all. It proved his worth to North, helping compensate for his lack of combat experience.

Matthew had spent his three tours of Syria on nothing but sentry duties. He never once discharged his weapon during the entire period, even on those brief chances when he stepped out on patrol. Of course, it didn't help him being a part of a UN support initiative to protect refugees, living under strict guidelines not to engage unless under immediate threat.

However, none of the rebels was stupid enough to risk doing anything of that nature. They knew the foreign troops were only temporary, like all the other volunteers who visited their home, thinking they could save them from the death that swept through. All they had to do was wait them out, and soon enough, they would leave on their own accord. Then, following years of supposed hard work in setting up the correct networks for refugees, they did, leaving the country no better off than when they first arrived.

In the months following his return to civilian life, Matthew had been stuck behind the wheel, delivering goods from warehouse to warehouse. He'd done crap in school. He left as soon as possible for the army with no real qualifications or skills that could transfer to other decent jobs. It meant he could never achieve a rank higher than Lance Corporal, and with the number of ex-service troops looking for employment, many of whom had far broader credentials than his, it was driving for him or nothing. It was the least he could do to pay his rent. Still, Matthew longed for something to make him feel like his life had some purpose beyond the daily grind of just living.

Fortunately, fate intervened for him when he heard David North was hiring for support on a last-minute rush job. Everybody was keen to avoid it, but Matthew leapt at the chance. North's reputation as a trigger-happy killer didn't phase him; instead, his tales inspired him. The man had once single-handedly defended a group of US Marines pinned down by enemy fire in the Hindu Kush and repelled their attackers. In another instance, he once infiltrated the Arab world and assassinated the head of a terrorist organisation in his own home. It's a crime they refuse to admit ever happened, even to this day, since they want to avoid any awkward conversations about why they were shielding a known terrorist. The stories created an impression that North was a living legend. The chance to work with him on just one job would give Matthew vast amounts of credibility in his search for military work. He'd then be able to put his true talents to use and finally feel like he was living instead of simply surviving. Even if working with someone like North resulted in that for him, he would gladly bear that cost, whatever it may be.

Matthew was about halfway into the Glock when he had to stop due to his mobile vibrating away in his pocket. He fished it out to see what was happening and was stunned to see the news notification announcing the home secretary's death.

It was public.

He scrolled through the report and became a tad nervous. He knew the entire country would find out eventually but didn't think it would happen this quick, given how North had only killed him thirteen hours ago.

Matthew turned around to gauge North's reaction, except there weren't any. North sat at his table without a care in the world. He was busy inspecting the wiring on a bunch of small explosive packs they'd collected from one of his connections. He'd laid enough out on the table to obliterate the room they were sitting in twice over. It wasn't something Matthew was keen on using. However, as North had put it, they were his insurance plan if things turned to shit, and given how this entire thing was a rushed job, he predicted it would.

Matthew guessed he wasn't aware of the news and decided it would be wise to inform him, so he stood up and crept towards him.

North stared up at Matthew's approach, irritated by his interruption.

"It's become public," Matthew remarked gently, trying not to agitate him further.

North stared at him for a moment before he lifted his wrist, glancing at his watch.

"Hmm, earlier than expected, but no need to panic," he said, lowering his watch as if he just wondered what the time was.

Matthew stared back, somewhat baffled. He knew the risks of North's plan. He'd given him the rundown once he hired him. They were going into this half-blind, killing multiple government employees for an old comrade of his, possessing no details beyond their names, while they waited for the employer to come through with the rest of the info.

It's why he hired him straight away. North needed the extra support, not having the time to perform his regular prep work of scouting the target locations and doing a detailed attack strategy. North was making it up as he went along, given the deadline was just one day. It was why they took the trip to Liverpool once they learned the secretary wasn't returning to the capital but staying on for additional meetings. It wasn't an ideal way to operate for anyone, given who they were hunting, but the money they stood to collect was far too high to ignore.

Still, Matthew expected they would have a bit more breathing room before everyone in the government came after them.

"Doesn't this change the plan, though?" he pleaded. "I mean, they're probably already searching for us. Hell, they could come for us right now," Matthew said, trying to persuade him otherwise, to see his point. However, he only failed, agitating North further, who looked at him with a stern glance as if he were his teacher, disappointed in him for shouting out in class.

"No, it doesn't. They were always going to be searching for us, but it won't matter. I now have all the details on the second target, and with my strategy, finding us won't be a problem, so we press on until I say otherwise. Is that clear?"

Matthew had to stop and reaffirm his faith in North's reputation for high-stake contracts and how he'd consistently delivered on them. No matter how dangerous the missions were, he finished them, regardless of those he killed. Still, he felt he had to raise his concerns, even at the risk of angering North. He'd never been used to working in such hazardous conditions. They always backed his assignments in Syria with at least a dozen other soldiers, ready to assist at the mere sign of trouble, but he didn't have that here. It was just him and North, with a list of names of random citizens, with no sense of where they were apart from somewhere in London.

"Yes, but you said your employer had only given you bits of information on the targets. . ."

Matthew didn't have time to finish his plea as North raised his palm for him to stop. He could tell from his face that he'd grown weary, listening to him drone on about the same useless point.

"That is not a concern of yours. The employer will come through since this isn't my first stint with him, and believe me; he's desperate for these pricks to be dead before the sunsets. Therefore, you can close your lips and stick around for the glory this job will bring or you can pack your shit and piss off! Yet do so, with my reputation; I'll see that your name gets blacklisted from any military or security work until the end of time itself. Is that understood?"

Matthew stood frozen in his tracks, unsure of what to say or whether to speak at all.

"I said, is that understood!" North repeated more aggressively, wanting his response.

Despite Matthew's concerns about its appearance, he had faith in North. Above everything else, he craved to get out of the crappy state of his life and knew this was it. This was the last chance he ever had at a meaningful life for himself, so he was determined to take it, even with all the risks attached.

"Understood, sir," Matthew said, bowing his head in apology. North grinned, knowing he would remain loyal to him and keep any future concerns he had to himself.

"Good. Back to work, then. Once Steve arrives with my gear, we move on to the second target."

Matthew retreated to his table as he resumed cleaning the Glocks, trusting his entire future to the care of the man sitting behind him.

Chapter 7

Eight people crammed into the back of a van designed for six will never be a convenient place for anyone. Still, it was just another day in the trenches for the counter-terrorist specialist firearms officers. Since becoming the Section's lead field agent, Ripley has worked with numerous members of CTSFO on countless missions. She trusted them with her life and vice versa. No matter how volatile or dangerous the situation appeared, each officer had earned their spot to be here in this van. They knew how to handle themselves, having the utmost discipline in their work. So, a little cramped space wouldn't cause them a single bit of fuss.

Ripley sat parked in an Audi A3 beside the van, inspecting the warehouse where they had tracked North's vehicle to. From what she could tell, it was just another old factory rotting away, waiting for someone to put it out of its misery. Ripley couldn't spot anything amiss aside from the decay. It seemed all clear, with no guards or spotters watching the yard. Inside, though, it would be a different story. They didn't know what to expect or how many people might end up wounded or, perhaps, killed once they stormed in. It's the same risk Ripley or any member of

CTSFO face whenever they enter an unknown location, where threats lurk around in any direction, ready to pounce.

You could have all the training in the world, but it can't ever predict what you'll face. All you could ever do was rely on the person beside you and face the situation united, hoping for a bit of luck that you'd make it out alive.

Ripley sat for a short time, as she had throughout her life, pondering the situation. She weighed up her options, the risks they might face if they entered now unprepared, compared to the delays they might face while they waited. She could monitor the building for hours, hoping to spot a clue about what was happening inside. Perhaps this may or may not give her the edge needed to ensure the safety of her team, but she'd never know, not until it was over. She thought it all, though, piece by piece as she stared up at the warehouse, scanning it over once more. She assured herself that she'd overlooked nothing that could pose a threat to the officers next to her.

After a few more seconds of consideration, she reached for her radio, settling on her course of action. It was time to enter.

"Commander, it's a green light. Move in now!" she barked.

The van's back door burst open in mere seconds of the order echoing out. The team poured out, charging straight towards the building at a breakneck speed, their SIG716 rifles scanning every inch of the building. Fingers rested on triggers, primed to fire at any threat that may pop out, with Ripley behind them every step of the way.

It took less than nine seconds before they reached the front door, and the team spread themselves around it. After a dozen seconds with no sign of bullets flying at them, the commander, who stood in front, signalled for them to burst open the door. One of his team stepped forward not long after, wielding a massive metal ram. She approached the door while the rest covered her, watching the warehouse for signs of attackers. Once in position, she heaved the ram with all her strength and slammed it into the door. The impact resulted in both hinges blowing clean off as the entire team poured into the warehouse one after the other.

After entering, it was clear that the entire building seemed abandoned. There was nothing inside except what lay in the middle of the vacant space. It may have had a thick sheet over it, but there was no hiding; it was a vehicle. Once the team had cleared the rest of the warehouse, finding nothing, Ripley signalled them to approach the mysterious vehicle surrounding it. Almost anything could lurk underneath the sheet, waiting to surprise them, so it was safer to have some precautions on hand to deal with it.

Once in position, the commander glanced towards Ripley, signalling that he was moving in himself to inspect what lay underneath. He crept forward, one foot at a time, keeping his ears open for anything out of the ordinary. He anticipated a counter once he grabbed the sheet, but nothing happened. It remained unnaturally silent as the moment for attack passed by without incident. Then, after a brief pause, he glanced at Ripley for approval. She tightened the grip on her pistol, nodding for him to remove it. The man took a deep, long breath to calm his growing trepidation and yanked the sheet off with all his strength.

Everyone was on edge. The officers held their fingers over the triggers, waiting for any sign of a threat, but there wasn't any. Instead, as the sheet fell to the floor, it revealed the mystery vehicle as an ordinary BMW. Still, it was the same one North had used last night.

From the outside, the vehicle appeared abandoned as the commander peered through the windows, beaming his flashlight inside, but, to his relief, he found it empty. There were no signs of foul play or obvious booby traps of someone waiting inside to murder them. Instead, all he saw were piles of disused sweet wrappers of every known brand as he shined his light over them.

The commander's nerves weakened as he kneeled below the vehicle, finding nothing but fragments of dust particles underneath. He triple-checked his findings, shining his light across every part bolted on the undercarriage, from the drive shafts to the undertray. He inspected each panel mounted on, the brackets used in between, and every screw, nut, and clamp used to fix them all in place. The commander made sure he missed nothing that would pose an immediate risk to those around him at all times. Then, after a few minutes, he stood tall, finding no traps of any kind, as he moved to the front of the vehicle to further examine it.

The team remained steadfast. They were ready to pounce on any surprises that might still lie in wait for them. However, as every second of silence wore on, it became apparent that nothing would arise. The commander found no evidence of threats from inside, just an endless supply of rubbish and wrappers tossed between the seats, like in any other car.

Nothing seemed out of place within the vehicle, so the commander stepped closer to check the interior. He felt more relaxed than he'd been as his nerves settled. He pressed on the door handle and gently pried it back; to his surprise, it was still open. He waited a couple of seconds, listening for anything amiss, waiting for something to happen like usual, but again, nothing happened. It was silent.

All signs pointed to it as an ordinary vehicle that had turned up out of nowhere, so he kept pulling, thinking nothing more, but he was wrong. He was totally and utterly wrong. It wasn't until he peeked his head inside that he realised how short-sighted he'd been. He noticed the faint flashing light shining from under the passenger seat as his eyes drew closer to it. After so many years on the job, he knew what it meant. North had indeed set the vehicle to explode, and despite all his constant checks, he had caught him out, like the fool he was.

It wasn't clear how long he had, but he figured it was mere seconds upon hearing the terrifying sound of it activating. It was probably from a delayed time pressure switch, programmed to blow once the doors were open.

In the last seconds of the commander's mortal life, he didn't think of the son he wouldn't share a beer with once he turned eighteen. He also didn't consider the girl to whom he wouldn't be able to confess his true feelings, let alone his own life. Instead, he only thought of his team. He had a duty of care to safeguard their lives, no matter the situation. Therefore, instead of dashing away, hoping to survive, he buried his spiking nerves and threw the door back, leaping onto the bomb, hoping to reduce its impact. He then screamed at the top of his lungs, *"BOMD!"* But, as his voice filled the room, it activated.

The blast ripped out, catching everyone off balance. Those who reacted faster dived to protect themselves. Others leapt into the air, doing whatever it took to avoid the consuming flames. The blast incidentally engulfed the commander in a flash. Still, it wasn't such a quick or graceful demise for the rest of the team. Those closest to the vehicle suffered the most. The fire washed over them, melting the fabric off their clothes and sticking to their skin. All the training they knew disappeared into the smoke-filled room as they shrieked like wounded animals from the pain. They scrambled across the ground at breakneck speed, trying to extinguish the flames as fast as possible. The lucky ones who weren't burning to a crisp picked themselves up when they could stand. Then, as quickly as possible, they rushed over to help their friends before their skin deteriorated and they lost all aspects of who they were.

Ripley escaped the flames with no severe burns on her body, unlike the others howling in agony around her. Still, as she regained her balance, staring at the burning vehicle in front, a single thought grew in her mind amid the screams. It was a dark, disturbing thought that grew louder as she tried to ignore it.

These deaths are on me.

Chapter 8

Steve was barely into his twenties as he took his first steps into the loft, hoisting a rucksack across his back. He seemed a little agitated, browsing across the room before locking eyes on Matthew, who was finishing reassembling the Glocks he'd dismantled. He glanced up at the stranger, smiling. Steve did the same, relaxing his nerves on seeing a friendly face. However, it didn't last long once Matthew gestured him over in North's direction, hinting that it wouldn't be wise to keep him waiting.

Steve adjusted his gaze towards North, and for a moment, he paused, taking a deep, long breath. He hushed his anxiety deep down underneath a thick layer of emotion before stepping forward, one foot at a time. Despite his youthful appearance, he walked with stride and discipline, a by-product of a post-military career where you're still adjusting to civilian life. The army spends months upon months drilling into you on parade grounds the correct way to walk, act, stand, and carry yourself. No matter how soaked you are, how tired you may feel, or how late in the day it is, you'll have no choice but to take it in your stride and march on, just like the soldier you want to be. It's not the place for slouches' to exist in Her Majesty's military and never will be.

As Steve walked up behind him, North sat plugged into his laptop, busy mulling over his strategy. He stood at attention, waiting to be noticed, wondering if he should tap his shoulder, cough, or voice his presence. Still, he decided against it once he extended his hand out, realising he wouldn't have dared interrupt his commanders when they were working. It was something he didn't think should change with North, who was far more accomplished than any of them. So instead, he drew his hand back, remained at attention, as any loyal soldier should, and waited, knowing he'd see him in due course.

A few seconds passed before North felt the gaze of eyeballs glaring into him and glanced around to check on who it was. He tossed off his headphones, closed his laptop, and twisted towards him when he saw it was Steve.

"Took your time, Steve. Have you found what I was looking for?" North asked.

"I have the clothes you requested, Sir," he said, softer than expected, trying to hide that he felt somewhat uncomfortable in North's presence. Still, he held his nerve well while North peered into his eyes, waiting as he unhooked the rucksack and held it out. North snatched it out of his grip as he opened it up to inspect his purchase. He pulled out a pair of overalls with a fresh shirt and necktie tucked underneath. He then found the rest of the suit below as he studied the quality of each of the pieces.

"This should do the trick. Good job, Steve."

This small notion of gratification caused Steve to beam with delight. Like everyone, he'd heard of North's reputation as an aggressive, controlling type of person in his work. He was the sort of person who would willingly shoot people in the head for their mistakes, no matter how small they were. Due to this, there was a nagging worry in his mind over what would happen to him if he messed up the first task. He knew it would cast him in a negative light, potentially messing up his money or losing out on the job altogether if he didn't just take his life. Still, the fact he was complimenting his work meant he must have done something right, and for him, that was all he needed to keep his worries at bay.

North folded the clothes back inside. Afterwards, he pried a piece of paper from his back pocket and handed it over.

"Your next assignment."

Steve took the paper slowly out of North's palm to avoid tearing it. Once he opened it, he saw it was just three addresses he'd scribbled down.

"You'll head to the above address to pick up transport under the name of Derry. Once there, you'll proceed to the second one to collect a sealed package that an old mutual acquaintance of mine left there. It'll be open, so load it up and continue to the last address, where you'll wait until called. Is that clear?"

Steve looked back at him with delight. It was a relatively simple task, pick up and deliver. He was glad to have it as his first real paid job back, given how he was less likely to screw it up. He knew that if he did this without fault, it would aid in building his name, expanding his connections to land more regular work. It was something he badly needed.

In recent months, he'd taken a severe nosedive in terms of paid freelance work once that initial burst of goodwill he had on returning home dried up. He knew if he didn't act fast enough, nothing would happen for him, especially when the latest batch of ex-soldiers arrived home and joined in his search for the same type of freelance work he was after. From that point, chances of him securing anything would automatically fade away once dozens of the same qualified individuals fought over themselves, trying to land the same job. It's why he jumped at the chance once this opportunity with North presented itself to him. Yes, he probably wanted someone with more calibre, who's a bit more on his level in terms of skill and experience. However, since this was a last-minute rush job, North didn't have the luxury of picking the right candidate and had to settle with who he could get. Still, in doing so, Steve now had it. It was the chance he needed to relaunch himself and push his career forward once more to achieve genuine success.

"Don't worry, Sir, I won't fail you," Steve said with the utmost confidence in himself.

North stood up, placing his hand on Steve's shoulder, gently patting him as a sign of respect for his devotion.

"About nine hours from now, you'll have a year's salary the taxman knows nothing about." North stopped patting, gripping Steve's shoulder as he leaned in close to ensure nothing got lost in translation. "Only if you follow my instructions, that is. Otherwise, you'll be another dead man in the obituaries no one gives a shit about. Is that clear?"

Steve took a moment to absorb what he just said as he stood fixed in his stance, unable to turn away from North's piercing gaze. Then, with a quick nod, he agreed, embracing his stern attitude. Steve didn't want to appear as though he was having doubts and wanted to remain a team player, willing to do whatever was necessary for him. He may have felt uneasy about being a part of a David North plan, knowing people would die today, but that didn't matter. He wasn't involved in that side. As far as he saw it, that was North's doing and North's alone. All he needed was to focus on his assignment, and he'd be fine.

North smiled in response to his answer, releasing his grip as he patted him one last time. He knew Steve would do as required and fulfil his plan without a fault. North stashed his laptop away in the rucksack before picking up his explosives and walking to Matthew while Steve trailed him from behind. He placed both bags on the table, grabbing one of the reassembled Glocks and cocking it back. The motion was smooth and flawless, displaying zero signs of jamming up once it came to press the trigger. Next, North attached his silencer to it before loading a magazine, flipping the safety on, and tucking it away. He then turned to Matthew, who waited with bated breath for his response. North took his time, waiting a few seconds before he reached out and patted him on the shoulder to assure his compliance.

"Good work Matthew. You've done well."

Matthew lit up with relief. He figured North was moving on from their brief spat and was keen to carry on as they had.

"It's my pleasure," he replied.

North smiled, seeing that Matthew would stick with him as he predicted. He knew, as did Steve, that his offer was too compelling for either of them to turn down. He patted Matthew one last time before addressing the pair of them. "Both of you grab one. It's time for us to get started."

Matthew grabbed a Glock and passed it back to Steve, who was reluctant to accept it. It was something North spotted as he turned to address him.

"You're doing a job for me today, Steve, so you'll need some insurance. Trust me on that," he said, gesturing at the pistol.

Steve gazed at it for a split second before grabbing a magazine off the table, loading it, and tucking his weapon away in the back of his jeans. "I understand," he stated with passion in his voice. No matter how much he hoped, he wouldn't have to use it today on an innocent civilian. Still, he made sure neither of them would notice.

"Good, it's time to move then," North said, grinning back, trusting his team as they headed out onto the next stage of his master plan.

Chapter 9

Outside the warehouse, emergency services vehicles lined the yard with fire crews who, after an eleven-minute battle, had extinguished the huge colossal fireball inside. Paramedics attended to the wounds of every officer caught in the blast. However, in spite of their best efforts, over two-thirds of them would have third-degree burns for the rest of their lives, and they were the ones who escaped the brunt of it. For those who failed to escape the fire, their bodies had to be wheeled off to the nearest hospital, about seven miles away, for treatment. The flames had torn through layers of skin in no time, cutting into the tissues and dissolving the muscle.

In comparison, those closest to the fire had already reported deep-seated bone damage. However, their level of trauma had one saving grace: none of their nerve endings was intact, so they didn't suffer nearly as much as those around them. Even so, their screams still reverberated throughout the whole warehouse. Nobody knew if they would even survive the seven-mile trip to the hospital, let alone the countless surgeries that would follow them for life. Still, those who remained weren't so optimistic once they saw the remains of their charred bodies. It was clear from the patches of hair left behind, the level of skin still on their flesh, and the utter fear in their eyes. They realised it might be a blessing if they didn't survive in a kind and merciful way since it would spare them from a lifetime of everlasting pain. It was an uncomfortable truth no one wanted to admit aloud, but something they all shared.

Ripley and a few others were among the fortunate ones. The paramedics still checked them over as a precaution, but they'd survived the ordeal with no lasting injuries or burns. Ripley's body was still shaking from the blast, but she ensured nobody noticed. This wasn't the first explosion she had survived, and, to be honest, she didn't believe it would be her last. Nevertheless, she needed to remove it from her mind and work on the real problem of stopping North. She owed the officers who died around her that much. Otherwise, all the agony, the screaming she heard as the flames ate into their flesh, would have been for nothing.

North's chances of repeating this carnage in a more public setting were high. They had heard rumours he was trying out make-shift explosives similar to this to murder some of his prey but could never confirm it; until now, that is. The Section combined this with the notion that North, in his growing age, had reached a point where he honestly didn't care how many civilians ended up in his crossfire anymore. As long as he murdered his target, he would be fine.

It played on her mind while Ripley paced over the wreckage, keeping herself centred on the mission. The 3 Series was still the Section's only active connection to North. The only problem was that he'd burnt it to a cinder, so whatever leads it could've provided were now lost. Even so, Ripley wasn't ready to dismiss it yet. She suspected North set this trap to throw them off his scent, keeping himself out of sight as he did whatever he came here for. Despite this, a thought kept playing around her mind that if North wanted to cause maximum casualties, he could have wired the doors to blow once they stepped inside. It led her to suspect there was something more to the vehicle. Perhaps there was a clue left behind that could help her. She knew it was a long shot, though, considering it was just as likely North was deliberately trying to mess with them, the heartless bastard he was. Still, Ripley wasn't signing off on their sole connection to him until they inspected every inch of the vehicle. She had called for a forensic unit to arrive once the flames subsided. The clock was ticking and anything they found, no matter how insignificant it seemed, was a potential lead to North's whereabouts.

Forty-two minutes passed with no developments as the forensic teams made their way through the wreckage. They salvaged a few bits and pieces of the explosive package, but nothing was readable due to the blast. Any clues it could have provided to who produced it disappeared without a trace. In the meantime, Ripley paced around the vehicle, assessing her next move and concentrating on the problem at hand. Her mind raced back and forth with itself as a series of thoughts after thoughts popped into her head. They ranged from widening their current search radius to chasing down all witnesses who may have noticed something. Alternatively, she could search through all the cameras surrounding the warehouse and beyond, hoping that one of them captured an angle on

North's movements. Even though she knew, deep down, how improbable it was since they trained North as hard as her in counter-surveillance, it came naturally to him. He knew better than anyone how to disguise himself from public view by not wearing anything flashy and only using back alleys to move around in. He also lived in places with minimal security where they wouldn't dare question another random face. These were mainly homeless shelters and doss houses, where he could easily blend in with the crowd, stay hidden, and murder his victims with ease.

North was a ghost; he had been for the last eight years plus. So, finding him in a city of over nine million was next to impossible. However, it wasn't until a forensic team member placed part of the burnt-out license plate next to her did a credible idea popped into her mind. It was one that only she would have known about as she caught sight of the dealership's name below the reg. Ripley froze in her tracks as she tilted her gaze into the wreckage, not knowing why she hadn't come to that conclusion sooner. She quickly threw on a forensic suit to approach the charred remains without contaminating them.

Ripley knew what she needed to find as she scrutinised the interior frame of the vehicle. It wasn't clear to the rest of the team what she was looking for, but no one bothered to stop her. They figured it was best to carry on with their assignments and let her be since she was on the lookout for something in particular. Ripley focused her gaze on each door frame as she carefully examined them. She studied every dent, mark, and piece of damage engraved into the metal to ensure she missed nothing before tackling the remaining blown-out doors, repeating the same method to guarantee nothing went unchecked. She slid her fingers all over the metal, feeling every crack within it until she found what she'd been looking for. It filled her with glee as she rubbed the unnatural shape on the bottom edge of one of the rear doors. There was something hidden in the corner behind the remains of the door seal. It was the sort of thing no one would ever think to check without first putting your head on the ground to view.

Ripley dropped to the floor to view her find, but it was impossible to identify due to all the fire damage and muck covering it. Still, as Ripley continued to touch the shape, sensing its rough edges and the oddness of the design, there was no doubt in her mind that the fire couldn't have formed it. In addition, it couldn't have come from the door being scraped or struck against something; instead, it must have come from another source. At least that was what Ripley was counting on. She immediately sprung up, walking over to one of the forensic members on the ground, documenting the interior wreckage of the vehicle with her camera.

"Hi there," Ripley said, bending down, meeting her on her level.

"Hey, did you find what you're looking for?" she asked, facing her.

"Not quite. Look, I know you're pretty busy with the wreckage and everything, but if you can spare me a few minutes, I'd appreciate your help confirming something for me."

The forensic member smiled and nodded without hesitation, more than happy to assist as Ripley extended her hand out for her.

"Alright, let's see what you got." The member took Ripley's hand, getting to her feet as the two of them, walked over to examine the mark.

"I need you to do whatever you can to clean this up to determine what type of mark this is," Ripley asked as the woman lowered herself to examine it.

"Give me a few minutes. I'll see what I can do for you."

The woman took out a range of brushes and materials to disinfect the selected area. She then started scraping the muck, layer by layer, taking care not to leave any of her marks on the engraving for fear it would become illegible. After that, she switched between her tools, hacking at the grime with each swipe.

Ripley, in the meantime, stood behind, arms crossed, twitching her fingers over her elbow. She waited in anticipation for the member to give her the exact answer she needed to hear right now as she watched her slowly peel back the muck, one piece at a time.

It took several long minutes before the forensic member felt satisfied with her efforts to take the pictures and show them to Ripley. Still, she'd done it, thanks to a bit of luck and some hard graft. The women had finally removed enough of the muck to reveal the engraving *L.R.4.* in the metal. It caused Ripley to beam with delight as she stared at the image, turning to the forensic member and squeezing her hand with a gentle smile.

"Thank you! I can't tell you how much this helps."

The woman politely smiled back. "Just glad I could help," she proclaimed, unaware of this little find's significance.

Ripley dashed out of the warehouse, ripping her forensic suit off and tossing it on the ground before jumping into her Audi and driving off.

Her lead on North was now secure.

Chapter 10

Ripley drove across the capital for almost twenty minutes before stopping in front of a car lot crammed with a variety of second-hand vehicles. It was awash in Fords, Toyotas, Astras, and every other model you can think of to buy at a reasonable price. All of them were in pristine condition. There were no dents, scratches, or other imperfections customers would love to whine about if given half a chance to help lower the asking price that bit more. A massive, luminous banner waved above them all, something you would be hard-pressed not to spot for miles. It advertised a once-in-a-lifetime sale on selected vehicles, but only if you were to buy this week and this week alone.

Ripley had zero interest in buying one; that wasn't why she was here. Instead, she had come to see the owner, Mr Kieran Page. She'd met him a couple of months ago after discovering he was supplying vehicles under the table to certain members of the criminal underworld. The story was that if you wanted a decent motor with no outstanding record, that wouldn't have any physical connection to you: *"go see Mr Page, and he'll sort you right out."* He should be rotting away in some prison cell instead of sitting in his office with a warm mug of Earl Grey. Ripley had gathered enough information on him to ensure he'd go down for years after catching him supplying getaway vehicles to an extremist zealot group she was tailing. However, once the cuffs were on, he had a massive change of heart, wanting to make amends for his crimes by serving his country.

In exchange for not throwing him into a cell and leaving him in peace to run his business, he agreed to keep a detailed mental record of all vehicles sold under the table. It was a record that only he and Ripley would ever know existed. In all fairness, though, it was a decent deal that served her well since it gave her an inside track into criminal activities.

It doesn't matter if the selected vehicle had undergone a makeover, had a fresh coat of paint, changed its plates, or added meaningless pounds' worth of aftermarket accessories to disguise itself. Thanks to the hidden engraving within the frame, Ripley could always trace it back to Kieran's business, no matter where it came from. It could be a beachfront parking lot, some random train station in the east, or a backstreet in the heart of London. All she needed was to find the hidden code in the metal to determine if it was one of his or not. Likewise, since there were so many cameras surrounding the lot, Ripley always had a decent chance of discovering who owned the car.

For Kieran, it was the most desirable outcome he could have wished for. As soon as his clients found out he was in prison, the question they'd all be asking themselves was: *did he sell us out?* It's fair to say none of them trusted a man like him to keep quiet. He spends every day of the week saying whatever bullshit comes out of his mouth to convince people to buy his motors. Therefore, it was no surprise to hear that he was so desperate to avoid prison, given how there was no guarantee he would walk out alive.

Ripley exited her vehicle, scanning the area as she crossed the street. It was quiet as she walked up to the office block, pushing the door open. Inside it was the same, no customers waiting for service or phones ringing on repeat. It was apparent the sale wasn't working as he'd hoped, but Ripley preferred it that way, as it reduced the chance of anyone interrupting her.

She was half expecting to be greeted by some receptionist eager to help sell a motor. Instead, she had to contend with some young girl who was too busy on her mobile liking some celeb's posts to notice that someone had just walked in. Her service skills needed significant improvement if she hoped to move beyond this desk, but Ripley brushed it off. She wasn't here to see the receptionist but the man sitting at the desk behind her. It wasn't difficult to spot Kieran as he always wore expensive Italian suits every time she met him, that contrasted with everything else in the office. It never seemed to bother him, though. Kieran was the sort of man who preferred the finer things in life, with his Omega watch and Gucci shoes that cost more than most monthly salaries. He was a staunch believer in that age-old theory: *if you look the part, people believe you're the part.* All to create the perception to every customer who steps inside that they weren't getting some slacker who just needed a job, but a high-class salesman who'd sweep them away with his wit and charm. It was the main reason he sold to his underworld clients, as the income helped buy the suit he wore and all the others hanging in his wardrobe.

Kieran was busy writing something down on his pad, so it took him about six seconds to realise someone had walked in. He looked up, smiling, thinking he would greet a new customer, but his smile vanished as soon as he locked eyes with Ripley. They stared back at one another for quite some time before Kieran flinched and adjusted his gaze towards the girl at reception.

"Hannah, why don't you take an early lunch?" he suggested. The girl, however, took no notice of his request, staring at her phone, busy texting away, so Kieran repeated himself louder. "Hannah, lunchtime, leave us, please."

The girl heard him that time, finally looking up at Ripley, who ignored her gaze, while she continued staring at Kieran in case he attempted something stupid. Hannah's eyes flickered briefly at the pair of them before she shrugged to herself, realising whatever the situation was between them had nothing to do with her. She was nothing more than a bystander and had no role to play in this, whatever it may be, so instead, she just stood up and left the office.

"Alright, see you later, Unc," she said, still texting away.

Ripley stepped back, bolting the door with its safety chain to ensure no one was planning to disturb them. She then paced over to Kieran, who remained seated as he watched her every move.

"So, how's business these days, Kieran? Are you selling a lot of motors?"

Kieran replied with a smile, humouring her. "Well, I can't complain. Business is doing fine despite these troubling times."

A faint laugh escaped Ripley's lips. "I'm glad to hear, but now that the pleasantries are behind us, I need info on one of our special motors."

Kieran stared at her in resentment. "Well, I didn't think you were here to buy one, now did I? You know, when I made this arrangement, I don't remember the part where you could come and disrupt my business whenever you fancy."

A flush of frustration washed over Ripley, thinking he had any input in how the arrangement worked. She stood in front of his desk, staring at him, saying nothing. It made Kieran uneasy as Ripley was quite intense when enraged, especially after everything she'd endured in the last few hours. She could still hear the screams of those officers echoing in the back of her mind.

As the seconds passed by, Kieran became more and more uncomfortable as Ripley's gaze kept digging into him. He couldn't figure out where to look or if he should say anything, so he just slumped into his chair, listening to the seconds tick by on his thousand-pound watch.

After a few moments, Ripley kept the screams at bay, pushing them to the back of her mind as she concentrated on the mission, on stopping North.

"I don't have time for your bullshit today. Your deal with me keeps you out of jail and in these stylish suits you're so fond of. If you want that to stop, take the years inside, and pray to whatever God you worship that none of your clients decides to pay you, or your family, a visit," Ripley said, gesturing towards the photo on his desk, with whom she could only presume was his sister and phone-addicted niece. "But until that happens, you work for me, remember?"

Kieran stared back, biting his bottom lip, reflecting on the words about to leave his mouth. It took him a minute, playing them all over in his head, before he finally gave in to her. "Alright, what vehicle is it, then?"

Ripley cracked a smile. She knew above everything else Kieran's clients scared him shitless, for they were the sort of people who wouldn't let an incident like this pass unpunished. These are the types of people who have enough contacts and resources in prisons to locate him wherever he might be. It meant that he would do whatever it took to keep their arrangement under wraps for the rest of his life, however long that may be.

"Blue BMW, 3 Series."

Kieran bounced his fingers off his forehead as he started mulling over the countless clients it would relate to. After a while, he looked up as if a light bulb had just flickered on in his mind.

"Wait, are you sure it was a blue BMW?"

Ripley looked at him, thinking he was trying to be funny. "Yes, it was. Your tag was on the inside. Why, what does it mean?"

"The funny thing is, I remember that one because some guy bought it yesterday by the name of Derry or something fake like that. Either way, he bought two BMWs but left a down payment for a third vehicle to collect today."

Ripley was stunned beyond words as if she'd just caught North with his dick hanging out.

"When are they coming?" she asked, hiding the excitement in her voice, still maintaining her professionalism.

"They said someone would pick it up early lunchtime today." He glanced down at his watch, seeing it was almost noon. "So, I figure they should be here within the hour."

Ripley's mind flooded with wild, thrilling fantasies about catching North in the act within seconds. Finally, she would stop this madness of his here and now before he murdered anyone else today. However, all those fantasies soon turned into a sense of frustration once she collected her thoughts, remembering how Kieran said *"someone"* would pick it up. *"Someone."*

She realised North wasn't about to risk collecting it himself. He wasn't that stupid. Instead, he'll likely send a proxy, probably the same person who drove him around last night. In any case, it was still her chance to gain an inside track to finding him.

"Which one?" Ripley asked as she turned towards the window, scanning over the vast range of vehicles on display.

Kieran stood up, stepping next to her as he pointed towards the marked vehicle. "Black XC90 at the front, you see."

Ripley spotted the shitty old four-by-four Volvo parked out in the front. She stared at it, instinctively knowing the ideal course of action to take, as she turned back to Kieran.

"Alright, when this person comes to collect, you're gonna hand over the keys and just give it to them like usual."

Kieran looked back, confused. "Wait, that's all you want me to do?" he asked, thinking he might have missed something.

"Yeah, that's all you'll need to do. Also, while I'm here, I'll take the details of the other BMW if you'd be so kind."

Kieran was more than happy to accommodate her request if it meant getting Ripley out of his business as soon as possible. This was before anyone caught sight of her and started asking awkward questions; he knew he couldn't explain. He returned to his desk, scribbling down the details before handing them over.

"Alright, I will. These are the details, but the guy declined my offer for cloned plates, saying he had his own. So, this might not be of any use."

Ripley hid her frustration as she snatched the paper from his grip, knowing North was using the same trick she once pulled when she needed to disappear. She once bought an off-the-grid vehicle from one source but used the plates she had switched over from another car to craft a protective barrier. This meant that if the source started blabbing, everyone would hunt for the wrong vehicle, allowing her to stay hidden.

She tucked the piece of paper away in her pocket as she walked back towards the door, unlatching the chain as she left the office.

Kieran breathed a sigh of relief, watching her exit. He then settled back in his chair, carrying on with his business as if nothing had happened, ready to charm his next paying customer.

Ripley walked up to the Volvo and scanned her surroundings. After determining that no one was watching, she bent down and shuffled under the vehicle. She then yanked a small tracker from her pocket and tucked it into the undertray. Once she had locked it in place and made sure it was out of sight, Ripley slid out and wandered back towards her Audi. She kept a close eye on her surroundings, scanning for unusual behaviour, just in case the driver was anything like her and came earlier to check the place out.

Ripley whipped out her mobile when she was inside and dialled the Section.

"Harper, listen up. I've activated a tracker. The code is Alpha, Lima, Zulu 112. Do you have it?" she said, listening to him hit different keys on his keyboard.

"I have it, clear signal."

"Copy that. I'm sending you the details of another BMW North bought from my location. Unfortunately, the reg is no good, so you're better off trying to locate it via its make and model instead."

"Roger that. I'll start checking CCTV in the vicinity. What about you?"

"I'm following up on a new lead. Someone connected to North is due to collect the vehicle I've tagged, so I'm planning to stake it out and see if it leads me to the man himself."

"Good find. I'll inform Denver of your progress."

"Cheers," she said, hanging up and adjusting her seat back, hiding as well as she could, while she kept a watchful eye on the street, wondering who would arrive for the Volvo.

Chapter 11

Time moved at a snail's pace. It was unclear how long had passed since Ripley took her current position, given her refusal to glance at her wristwatch for fear of missing something. However, despite the steady footfall surrounding the lot, not a single person approached the office. The lack of interest didn't signify good odds for the success of Kieran's sale. Still, Ripley remained fixed in her position. She watched, scanning every individual's movement in her eye line, wondering if they were the one. Were they North's man? Or, with any luck, North himself.

It took another six minutes of non-stop staring before someone ventured into the office. The individual was male given his build but kept his head down as if he was trying to avoid any attention. It was difficult for Ripley to get a closeup of him as he entered. Even so, she kept her eyes fixed on the door, waiting to see what would happen once he stepped out.

If this was indeed her man, all Kieran had to do was give him the keys. She knew he wasn't stupid enough to risk tipping him off. No matter how much front he had, Kieran wanted to avoid a life in prison. He knew it was a death sentence for him and his family, something he'd never admit aloud to anyone, including himself.

After a couple of minutes of constant staring, the door finally opened. The guy strolled out of the office with Kieran, who pointed him towards the bottom of the lot, towards what she could only assume was the Volvo. Kieran then shook the gentleman's hands before passing the keys over to him and dashing inside should something arise. He knew Ripley had something in mind for him, so he wanted to distance himself from it as much as possible. He needed to avoid any potential blowback, for he knew whatever it was would come back to bite him someday.

The guy casually strolled around the lot, checking out all the vehicles on display, pausing next to the prized motor in Kieran's sale, a one-year-old C200 Coupe Benz. He couldn't help but admire the beauty in its design as he gazed, fantasising about owning one for himself. There are few things more exhilarating than doing ninety on the open road as you feel the wind rushing through your hair without a care in the world. Next stop anywhere, then everywhere. This world is yours to explore, so explore it. He patted the top of the bonnet, thinking to himself: *"One day. One day indeed."*

As he continued towards the bottom of the lot, he stopped next to the Volvo, pressing the fob to unlock it.

It was her man.

While he gazed around at the rest of the models on offer, she caught a glimpse of his face but failed to recognise it. It wasn't North despite her wishes. Still, it confirmed her theory that he was using a proxy, but whatever the case, this mystery person was now her most promising lead to locating him. The guy, however, didn't jump into the driver's seat; instead, he took a stroll around the vehicle. It wasn't clear if he was looking for a specific problem or just checking out the bodywork for dents as he examined it. The only thing she could gather about him was, from the way he carried himself, he had a military background, and judging by his youth, it was pretty recent. Ripley knew how to spot them from afar since she spent the entirety of her childhood around soldiers, thanks to her father's extensive military career.

The tales of his heroic actions, the lives he'd saved, and his successes inspired her more than any subject in school could. However, most of all, she learned about the true nature of life in the military, the sacrifices and hardships you'd have to endure to preserve life each day. It was something Ripley desired to be a part of her whole life. She wanted to safeguard her nation's citizens, just as her father once did, from those who intended to harm them.

It took the mystery guy a couple of minutes to examine the vehicle before hopping in the driver's seat, where he ran through a similar style of checks inside. Eventually, after a much quicker inspection, he seemed satisfied with the motor as he ignited the engine, driving off the lot. Ripley jerked her seat up, following him. The screen on her mobile lit up, showing the tracker on the move.

Ripley smiled, lifting the mobile to dial the Section.

"Harper, the vehicle's moving. Check you have a signal." She stayed silent, cutting into the next lane while listening to him typing away on his keyboard.

"Confirmed. It's a solid link from my end. I'll monitor the situation from here and advise you if anything comes up."

"Copy that. I'll report in when I have something," Ripley said, hanging up, placing the mobile on the dash, and switching it back to show the tracker's movement.

She joined the traffic, keeping a fair distance behind the Volvo to avoid spooking the driver. She didn't want to draw any attention to herself. With his military background, he would likely realise he was under surveillance and abandon his plans. Ripley thus kept her distance, allowing the tracker to do its job.

After almost ten minutes of navigating the city's streets, trying her best to keep three cars behind him when she could, the driver made an unexpected turn into an industrial yard. The move posed a problem for Ripley, who no longer had the luxury of traffic to mask her approach. Her only option was to pull further back, allowing him to get ahead so as not to alert him to her presence. Then, after thirty seconds had gone by, she followed him in.

With a pause in her stride, Ripley took a moment to examine her current location. She could quickly tell she was in a ghost town, given the run-down conditions of all the buildings she drove past. It meant that the sound of another vehicle would catch anyone's attention. Ripley, in response, eased off the accelerator, slowing much further down, before slamming on the brakes as the tracker stopped dead in its path. She didn't know why, but something felt off.

Ripley parked near one of the buildings, hiding her vehicle next to it as she fixed her eyes on the screen. Twenty seconds passed without her breaking concentration, yet the tracker remained frozen in place. The same thing happened for the next twenty seconds. Then, another twenty seconds after that, the same. It never moved, not once.

Multiple thoughts crossed Ripley's mind about what was happening. Still, she kept referring to the two most likely options, either the driver suspected someone was tracking him and ditched the vehicle, leaving it as a trap for her, or he instead came here to meet someone, perhaps North himself.

Ripley sat back, thinking it all over, before admitting that she wouldn't find any answers sitting still. She picked up her mobile and exited the vehicle, drawing her Glock. In a flash, Ripley raced over to the location on the tracker, where it remained frozen in place. She maintained a low profile, sticking to the walls to avoid being spotted by anyone who may be watching. Ripley didn't know what to expect and was keen to avoid walking into something she couldn't shoot herself out of. She crept slowly along the edge of the buildings, making as little noise as possible until she reached the spot where the tracker was coming from.

Once she reached the corner of one of the buildings, she glanced around, spotting the Volvo with its boot opened up. The mystery driver emerged from a storage unit carrying a large sealed package. It wasn't clear what the package was at her distance, but Ripley figured it wouldn't be anything cheerful, not with North's involvement. She didn't know him to be a charitable man, not unless it was about a quick death. Once the driver had secured it in the boot, he closed it down, pulling the shutters on the unit before stepping back into the vehicle, and reversing around.

Ripley jerked her head back and rapidly scanned her surroundings for something to hide behind. Luckily, the building she was leaning against was next to another warehouse. It meant there was a narrow gap between them, not much, but it would be fine for someone with Ripley's build. Still, she didn't have time to be fussy as she heard the vehicle coming closer and closer. The driver was heading back. If he were to spot her now, it would ruin the entire initiative, and then she'd never find North. So, Ripley concealed her Glock and dashed between the buildings, pushing herself into the narrow space, remaining still, like she was a part of the structure. Then, as if by magic, he never noticed her as he zipped past. It's probably because it never crossed his mind to be mindful of his surroundings, as you can never be too sure of when someone's watching you.

When she heard the engine fade out into the distance, Ripley unfroze and leapt out of the gap, sprinting towards her vehicle. There was no doubt this was just another pickup for him. Still, she knew that whatever was in that package had to be related to what North was planning.

Once Ripley reached her Audi, she hopped back into the driver's seat, glancing at her mobile. The tracker was still active. The driver hadn't found it, so he could still lead her to North.

With that in mind, she ignited her engine and chased after him.

Chapter 12

It took a couple of minutes, but Ripley caught up behind the Volvo. From the route he seemed to take, based on all the traffic signs she glimpsed, the driver was clearly heading into West London. She repeated the same motion, letting the traffic mask her approach as they travelled across the capital into Shepherd's Bush market. Then, after driving up and down various streets, he parked along the curb near the centre of the market.

Still tailing, Ripley followed suit and parked further back to avoid spooking him, ensuring she had an angle on him all the time. Finally, she killed her engine and sat, watching the driver relax in his seat. He did nothing except sit for nearly three minutes, flipping through the radio stations. He followed it with another four minutes of repeating the same actions, never changing his position except to gape at some woman's firmly curved arse who wandered by in a short skirt.

As the eighth minute ticked away, Ripley grew more concerned about his lack of movement or interest in anything outside of finding the ideal station to listen to — or another arse to fantasise over.

She wasn't sure what he was trying to achieve. However, as she examined her surroundings, trying to find some sense of a clue, she felt no better. She realised the situation had become much more complex.

It might have been nearing the end of lunchtime, but the market remained packed with punters, thanks mainly to the weather. Every stall was open with traders yelling like Del-Boy, trying to flog their goods to every passerby. People were out and about, doing their daily shopping and running errands, while others were just out, enjoying the sunshine while it was there. It made her think that if something similar to the carnage North produced in the warehouse took place here, countless innocent bystanders would suffer a similar fate. In any case, that wouldn't bother North, not as long as he got what he needed, regardless of the body count left in his wake.

Ripley became agitated, not knowing what would happen once visions of explosions setting off filtered into her mind. It devastated her to see the civilians around her torn to pieces like the ones she witnessed this morning. Still, it wasn't as harrowing to her as their screams, their cries as they wished for it all to end. She had to slam her head back to drive them away and refocus her mind, shaking off the doubt, reminding herself their lives depended on her.

She reached for her mobile, dialling the Section to see if they could shed some light on the matter. "Harper, this doesn't seem right to me. Do you have anything in my current vicinity considered a target, as I'm not seeing anything here?"

"No, I'm afraid not. Since you've been stationary for so long, I started cross-referencing your location with all the schedules I have access to for government events, but nothing is coming up."

Ripley paused, glancing at the driver, mumbling along to what was the first decent tune he'd found. She glanced again at her surroundings, hoping to spot something that might provide insight into why they were here. She scrutinised each of the building's names, posters on the wall for upcoming events, and all the faces walking past. She hoped something would click to help make sense of what was happening, but it was all the same. Nothing seemed suspicious or out of place. It was just an ordinary street in London, like any other, so Ripley sat still, pondering why the driver came here, what purpose it served North. But, in doing so, a disturbing thought crept into her subconscious despite her best efforts to keep it at bay.

Perhaps this entire time, the driver knew someone was watching him. Maybe Kieran had tipped him off, or perhaps he spotted her car on the road, and this was just one big scheme to distract her and the Section. In other words, all the time she wasted trailing him around London was for nothing, and North had already done what he came here for.

Ripley sank into her seat as the doubt intensified over how she could let something like this happen. Despite her best efforts, she failed the officers who died screaming under her watch and those still critical in hospital beds. It was her fault. She was supposed to stop it, and she'd failed.

Her first thought was to walk over to the Volvo, haul the driver out, and crack his skull to discover what he knew about North, hoping to salvage the situation. However, her moment of uncertainty suddenly shattered when she caught sight of his actions from the corner of her eye.

"He's just stepped out of the Volvo," she remarked, gazing at the driver, who'd finally emerged from the vehicle. He rubbed his stomach from side to side and glanced around the street. Ripley sank into her seat to avoid drawing attention to herself, but there was no need. After about ten seconds of casual glancing around, the driver appeared satisfied with how things seemed and walked into the market.

"The target's on the move. I'm in pursuit," she said, stepping out of her vehicle. "Harper, you need to keep digging. He has to have a reason for coming here. We're just not seeing it yet."

"Relax, my dear, I'll find it. Just focus on him."

"Don't worry, I will," she said as the doubt subsided, regaining her self-confidence, knowing her efforts weren't in vain as she followed the driver into the market.

Chapter 13

It turned out there was no need for Ripley to chase after him.
After about a forty-second walk, he'd entered the nearest outdoor
cafe, sitting down at a table outside. Ripley hung back to build
some distance as she watched him settle in before entering.
She kept her distance, trying to avoid drawing any unwanted
attention. Fortunately, the cafe attracted a crowd, thanks to its
half-price lunches, so another face among them didn't cause a
second glance from the driver. Ripley sat down a few tables away
from him and noticed that you could still see the Volvo from
this location. Whatever the driver was doing here, he wanted
to ensure the vehicle was always in his sight. She figured it had
something to do with the package inside the boot.

Ripley leaned back in her seat and pondered that the most
likely reason for him being here was for a handover. She watched
the vehicle, assessing everyone who came near it, anticipating
North's arrival, thinking he may show up in person to collect.
The only time she stopped looking at it all together was when
the waitress asked for her order. Ripley took a gander at the
menu before tossing it aside and opting for a plain cup of
coffee. She didn't care about her purchase, as she just wanted
the waitress to disappear so she could concentrate on her task.

The waitress smiled politely at her manners, as if they were second nature, and returned with the coffee in no time. A couple of minutes passed without incident before Ripley glimpsed the same waitress coming back with what looked like the lunchtime special advertised of breaded cod with chips. Given his choice of order, it seemed reasonable to assume she'd have to wait sometime for whatever would occur. The driver, meanwhile, wasted no time digging into his meal, like he hadn't eaten all day. Ripley guessed he must have got peckish staring at the cafe, not knowing how long he would have to wait for whatever would happen.

The minutes ticked by as the traffic of people entering the market grew by the hundreds. However, despite all the fresh faces, none of them approached the driver or Volvo in any meaningful way. Still, it did nothing to change Ripley's position. When working, she had laser-focused attention, especially when out in the field, since it was here that people relied on her the most to keep them alive. She'd discovered this the hard way during her time in the Balkans due to the entire region being a hostile hell zone. Hidden around every corner was the threat of being kidnapped, blown apart, raped, or murdered, to mention just a few. The fear of it taught her never to lose focus and stay centred on the mission, the lives she was protecting.

For whenever you let go of your focus, for whatever reason, no matter how crucial it may seem, it may cost you the one thing we hold sacred to ourselves, our mere existence. It's a notion that is truer than ever in combat.

Ripley took another sip of coffee as she felt her mobile vibrating away in her pocket. She yanked it out, seeing the red flash on the screen from the Section. It's a colour that never signified good news. Still, as she answered, she kept calm to avoid drawing any attention to herself.

"Hey babe," she said, all friendly, like a loved-up teenager, the opposite of Denver's tone as he spoke.

"Ripley, the situation has gone haywire. We've received a credible threat from North claiming he will detonate a high explosive in London if a list of MPs doesn't resign in the next few hours."

Ripley remained relatively stoic as her gaze shifted towards the driver. He was still eating away, unaware of her presence, as she sipped her coffee like nothing was amiss.

In a faint, calm voice, she replied. "Now, this all makes sense for what he's been doing. This explosive has to be the package his driver loaded into the boot. — Are we positive this is North and not some fanatic trying to take advantage of the current crisis?"

"Harper's vetting it as we speak; however, based on the details mentioned in the demands regarding the secretary's death, it could only be from his killer."

Ripley glanced around at the market, noticing its increasing crowds, the growing targets for North. "There are hundreds of potential victims here. I'm going to need support in case this turns nasty."

"We've scrambled a bomb unit with support officers over to your location, but they're seven minutes out."

"I understand but for all we know, the driver can trigger the explosive himself. If we wait or if armed officers spook him, we could have a repeat of the seven-seven bombing on our hands. I'm in the ideal position to take him out without creating a scene."

"I figured you'd say something like that. I trust your judgment. Proceed with caution and good luck."

"Copy that, chief." Ripley ended the call but kept the mobile pressed against her ear as she relaxed and stood up with her coffee. After that, she walked towards the driver, pretending to have an imaginary chat to misdirect his attention. On approach, he glanced at her but didn't give her any consideration as he swallowed another mouthful of chips. Instead, he ignored her stupid conversation about who was the best actor to have ever played The Doctor.

Ripley saw his lack of reaction and knew it was her chance to act. She gradually extended her hand with the coffee out as she pretended to catch her foot on the adjacent table. She then stumbled to the ground but made sure the coffee hit him square in the crotch.

The driver leapt up with speed upon impact, staring at the coffee dripping from his jeans.

"Oh, my god, I'm so sorry," Ripley said with enough sincerity to ensure he thought it was just a genuine accident as she moved in.

The driver kept calm, not raising his voice as he took his napkin to wipe himself down. "It's fine," he said, masking his anger at the women for being so careless.

"Please let me help. It's the least I can do."

Ripley stepped closer to him, acting quite apologetic, pocketing her mobile as she grabbed a handful of napkins, trying to help wipe the coffee stains off. It was something the driver didn't mind at all. On the contrary, he was delighted at the notion of a gorgeous redhead like Ripley touching him so tenderly. Even if his jeans were in the way, it automatically brightened his mood. Still, due to his lack of attention, he was unaware that Ripley was encroaching on his personal space. As she closed in, poised to strike, she noticed the handgun tucked away in the back of his jeans. Her original plan was to use hers, but since he had a weapon, it would be safer to disarm him first to avoid any unintentional shootings.

Ripley swiftly skimmed the other customers, who appeared too engrossed with their meals to pay attention to them, so they were fine. The driver, meanwhile, was too busy gazing into the sky, fantasising over Ripley, unzipping his trousers and playing with his genitals to notice anything happening around him. It meant that the chance to strike was ideal for her. Ripley stepped behind and smacked him in the back of his knee with her boot. The sudden pain caused him to tumble to the ground as she snatched hold of his pistol. She unhooked the safety as she propped it against his back, hiding it away from public view as best she could with her body.

"Try anything stupid, and I shoot," she whispered into his ear as she helped him back to his feet, trying to avoid causing a scene. Still, as usual, the people around were too busy wrapped up in their own lives to pay any significant attention to them and so missed all the excitement. The driver, meanwhile, dropped his head in shame, disgusted with himself for getting caught out so blatantly. It took him a moment with her drilling the pistol into him before he nodded in agreement.

Ripley tossed some notes on the table to cover the bill, adding a little extra for the mess, before yanking him away. "Come on. We're taking a gander at that Volvo of yours," she remarked as they exited the cafe.

Ripley walked right beside him, holding her free hand around his chest, bringing him close to conceal the pistol as they walked towards the Volvo. Fortunately, most people who glanced in their direction assumed they were an oddball couple, given how they held each other. In any case, it didn't stop Ripley from sizing them up to guarantee no one would pursue them. It had become her habit to suspect an attack from anywhere and everyone, so she was determined not to slip up now. There was too much at stake to fail.

Throughout their joint journey, the driver didn't utter a single syllable or make any effort at resistance. Even if he could, what use would it be? He knew it was all over as the woman kept him restrained, repeatedly digging his pistol into his ribs. He realised there was no sense in fighting back, as he didn't fancy another blow to the leg or a bullet in the kidneys.

Once they reached the vehicle, Ripley slammed him into the boot while keeping her grip on him for insurance if he attempted to escape.

"Raise the boot. Any funny stuff, the first-round pierces through your knee. The good one, of course."

Despite his hesitation, the driver nodded back and fished out the keys, raising the boot. Ripley glanced back and forth at the people behind, trying her best to keep the pistol out of view to avoid attracting too much attention. Once the boot was open, she saw the package in the back and released her hand from his chest, tightening her grip on her pistol.

"Open it up. Come on."

He stepped forward, tearing into the package, only to stop in sheer horror once he discovered the contents. An explosive device lay inside, covered in wires on top, with slabs of Semtex stacked underneath, primed and ready to blow. The driver tried to back away, except Ripley kept him on his heels, preventing him from running off. She examined the bomb, keeping calm, knowing the blast would engulf hundreds of nearby bystanders in a split second.

"How's it triggered?" she asked, digging the pistol deeper into his flesh.

The driver's entire demeanour had transformed into a nervous wreck as his eyes grew dimmer and dimmer with every passing second he stared fixed on the bomb.

"I . . . I don't know. — All North told me to do was park it here and watch over it," he said, struggling to keep himself together. His mind was in disarray as he saw himself disintegrating to ash from the massive explosive beside him.

Ripley stared at the sweat coming off his forehead, his eyes wide with horror, figuring he was likely telling the truth. Yet, she kept the pistol pressed into him as the sound of the sirens echoed down the street.

Ripley marched into the road, dragging the driver with her as she signalled for them to approach her. Once the officers arrived, Ripley knocked the driver to his knees, raising the pistol to his skull. She then drew out her ID badge and summed up the situation to the officers, never once lowering the firearm. Her form of insurance if the driver was to attempt anything foolish. After finishing, they cuffed him and started securing the growing cordon, pushing the increasing crowd of wandering eyes away.

Ripley advised them to keep members of the press out as long as possible to help reduce the sense of panic. She knew that if the bomb came out on Twitter instead of an official statement from the relevant authorities, trying to find North would just become far more complex. It was in her best interest not to broadcast that they had captured the bomb since it would only give North another advantage. It's a luxury they couldn't afford right now, given what North was threatening them with.

Ripley stepped aside, leaving the explosive for the professionals as the bomb crews stepped up to the plate. She let out a sigh of relief, holstering the pistol, thankful that she'd avoided a repeat of the morning's carnage. She felt a huge weight lift off her shoulders, confident that they were closer than ever to finding North. Ripley took a moment to digest it, gathering her thoughts before pulling out her mobile, beaming at the win as she called the Section to give them the update.

"Harper, the bomb is being secured as we speak. I'm heading back with the driver. From what I've gathered, he's military. It wouldn't have been that long ago based on his age, so he'll have a file. Could you find it for me?"

But Harper didn't respond. His line remained silent.

Ripley became somewhat concerned as she glanced at her mobile, seeing she hadn't lost the connection.

"Harper? — Harper, are you there?"

Another brief silence followed before he answered, finding the words to explain the news to her.

"Ripley, we've just learned that an aide discovered MP Janet Lee gunned down in the same style as the secretary. It was North, no question."

Ripley froze in her tracks, overcome with resentment at the news. She ended the call without saying a word, looking into space, pondering how. How? Then, gradually, she stepped back to take stock. However, her attention soon turned towards some random vehicle nearby, causing her to lash out. She smashed into it again and again for failing to stop what North had done, the life he'd just taken.

Chapter 14

London's renowned finance companies make hundreds, if not thousands, of deals each week alone, all from the comfort of their desks. They shape their clients' futures in their favour with a few strokes of their keyboards. This is in spite of the fact they rarely see them, know where their funds land, or what fraction of it will end up in their client's pocket.

Still, each of these companies will consistently rake in the money, year after year, producing enough revenue for their clients to keep them coming back for that chance to earn a little more. Of course, the same applies to their bosses, who'll continue to earn their cut no matter what economic hardship the world may face. However, like so many companies before them, they strive to save as much money as possible, cutting costs wherever they can. It's a pretty simple ideology. The less money that flows out the door, the more they find in their wallets for the crap they don't need, thus maintaining their growing wealth. Due to this mindset, many companies of their size will always employ the cheapest cleaning company around. After all, it is a proven way to save money through and through.

The bosses only care about having the toilets sparkling clean whenever they need to take a shit. They don't give a crap about who cleans it or if that person's earning less than the legal minimum wage. Due to this, not a single employee of Wealth Management Finance could give you the name of even one cleaner that works for them. Since they are just faceless background workers, they never need to interact or acknowledge. However, doing so crafted the perfect infiltration point for North to kill his second MP.

His employer's information stated that the second target agreed to meet with the finance director for a lunchtime meeting. North's plan was simple: sneak in, find the target, kill her, and sneak out before anyone would notice.

It was a foolish plan that, on paper, sounded ridiculous, but in reality, when you said it out loud to yourself, it was ludicrous even to attempt. Still, none of it bothered North. It was why so many people turned to him to eliminate the targets others wouldn't even consider, believing it was too intricate. North, though, never cared how suicidal the tasks were. For him, they were all part of the chase, that adrenaline rush, to find and murder his prey without ever being caught. It's a feeling that kept him alive and full of energy, more so than actual food. Even as the years piled on, it kept him motivated to define the odds others thought were impossible. Still, for him to get close to the MP, North would require the correct disguise, one he had thanks to his constant planning.

The overalls Steve had purchased this morning meant no one gave him a second glance as he stepped through the back of the service entry like any ordinary cleaner. He was so well-dressed that the actual cleaners didn't notice themselves, but none of them felt inclined to make a single comment about it, even if they did. Almost all of them couldn't understand proper English outside of someone telling them what to scrub or vacuum. It meant there was no chance they would speak out of turn. Still, it wouldn't even matter what they'd said. They had no one to report to, no bosses or managers, just themselves. Furthermore, they wouldn't dare interact with any of the proper staff if they believed he was out of place, in fear of losing their job. It meant North was just another blank face among the crowd of manual workers as he made his way into the building.

He'd used this simple trick in multiple countries over his career to locate his targets who were in public places. It never failed to work for him, and he didn't see why it would change now. It was a tried and tested tactic. The only difference was that no one had hunted him this viciously the other times he'd used this trick. Still, thanks to a lifetime of conflicts throughout the world, North had learned one of the trade's most valuable tricks: *The art of distraction.* Keep your enemy focused on something completely different so you can carry out your true mission.

North knew the entire country would have learned about the home secretary's death when this meeting happened. It wouldn't take them long to figure out it was him. Even with his talents, there's no way none of the cameras wouldn't have spotted him at the hotel. He's gifted but not invisible. They would hunt after him with everything in their arsenal this time. They would never let him go, not after killing someone so prominent in the public eye. Still, North was more than ready to use this to his advantage, crafting what he referred to as noise. In this case, the noise would be a massive bomb on the other side of London. One he could trigger with a single text if he sensed too much heat or needed a quick diversion when the time came to disappear.

He began with a small taster hidden in the vehicle he used last night to sell the full effect. He set it as a trap for the security forces to discover. North knew their procedures well enough, having helped make a couple of them. He left a bread crumb trail for them to track the vehicle, thinking they would have the inside track on him. Then, when his smaller version activated, butchering a lot of agents by tricking them into thinking they would be free from harm, it would show how much of a threat he posed to the public.

As soon as he informed them about his larger version, the security forces would have no choice but to shift their attention toward preserving life for the great British public instead of seeking him out. Due to this, it would allow him all the time he needed to slaughter his prey. All it required was a strongly worded statement to the government to prove the entire situation was genuine, with enough details and ridiculous demands to sell the notion. After that, when the dust settles, and they figure out what happened, all three of his targets will be dead; then, North will vanish again, just as he always has, but first, he needed to find the second target for that to happen.

He walked through the company with no checks or fuss, making his way into the heart of the building with the ID card he swiped from an inattentive, clearer outside. However, despite all his planning, he was unsure what floor the target was on. He also knew trying to coerce or manipulate another receptionist into blabbing it out like at the hotel would raise too many red flags. It's especially true in a place like this, where they actively train staff not to disclose sensitive pieces of information to random strangers, regardless of their charm. Still, he figured as the MP was meeting one of the finance directors, he'd likely encounter a person of that stature near the top floor. He, therefore, started making his way into the structure, using a mop bucket he'd plucked from a supply closet he raided. It helped sell his disguise more than the ID, as anyone who glanced in his direction took no notice, assuming he was just off to clean something up. Besides, most of them were too concerned with sorting out their own lives to notice or even recall seeing him, anyway.

It took him about eleven minutes of relentless searching through floor after floor before finding the target. He finally spotted her through the window in the door of one of the corner offices. It may have only been at an angle, but he recognised her facial features, having studied them all morning. She had dark blond hair, lobe ears, a nose the size of a baby's hand, and a small birthmark at the bottom of her right cheek. It was Janet Lee, no doubt. She was sitting in a private room across a small conference table, with whom North could only presume as the company's director. Still, it didn't matter who it was; just being in the same room meant he had to die. It was nothing personal, but North would need every second he could to escape once the bodies dropped, so there could be no witnesses. After one last scan of his surroundings, he found that the corridors, to his luck, were still empty. Everyone nearby was busy in their own offices, unaware of his presence. It was his moment to act.

Calmly, North pried open the door, stepping inside, mop in hand, wiping the floor to sell his disguise. Once inside, North surveyed the room, confirming only the two of them were there.

The director snapped at him in a boiling rage for interrupting his meeting. "What the hell are you doing here? Get out, right now!" he barked.

Yet, all North could hear was the sound of the door behind him locking. Within a split second of it clicking shut, North dropped the mop, whipped out his Glock, and fired a single round in the director's head. Blood gushed out from his skull as the bullet pierced through, hitting the wall behind.

His actual target sat frozen in shock, not knowing what to do with herself. She considered trying to shout out for help, hiding under the table, or even tackling the shooter to save her own life. Each thought and more hurtled around in her mind at a frantic speed but, it was all pointless. North's reflex skills were still as sharp as when he set out for his first tour in Iraq. By the time the director's body struck the ground, he'd already re-positioned his pistol on her and squeezed the trigger.

Again, it was another clean kill through the forehead, taking mere seconds before the body fell to the ground in dismay. North swiftly pressed himself against the door, Glock in hand, ready to repel any attack that might come his way. He peeked outside through the door window, watching. Five seconds ticked by, but nothing happened. Ten followed, yet nothing changed. It was the same after fifteen, then twenty, then thirty, and so on; nothing changed. There were no screams of panic, alarms buzzing away, or people dashing to apprehend him. It seemed no one had heard anything inside this room. He was in the clear. As he stepped back, a smug grin appeared across North's face as he admired his overalls. They were clean, free from any blood splatters that would raise an eyebrow. He then tucked his pistol away and picked up his mop, stepping out as the blood of his latest victims gradually dripped onto the floor.

He kept at the same pace as he had entered to avoid catching anyone's eye, but no one paid him a second glance as he passed office after office. And why should they? If he even crossed anyone's sights, they brushed it off with the same collective thought: *"Oh, he's just off to clean something,"* thinking nothing more than that.

Still, it didn't stop him from spending the entire journey to the ground constantly checking over his shoulder, studying people's reactions. He tried to spot anything that might suggest they were staring at him for longer than they should. However, everyone just carried on as usual, busy staring fixed at their screens, working away on whatever finance scheme they were cooking up to secure their fattening bonuses. Nobody was aware of his existence or any of the company's low-paid cleaners. It was something North couldn't help but smile about. He knew if they bothered to pay any serious attention to them, apart from the sporadic nods in the hallway, their director would still have his brain intact. It took him another seven minutes, but he made his way back to the service entry without difficulty. He was all clear. No one was coming after him or even aware that they should. North then propped his mop against the wall and exited as he entered, as though he had never been there, a feeling every cleaner knows all too well.

As North made his way onto the main street, he walked hand-in-hand with the crowd. He maintained a low profile and hid his face to avoid being detected by CCTV cameras, hoping to pin his location. He allowed the swarm of foot traffic to mask his presence as he headed down the sidewalk before breaking off into the back allies. After a few minutes of casual walking through various side streets, he further distanced himself from the company. Then, after about half an hour of wandering, he found Matthew waiting patiently for him at the agreed rendezvous point. His hands gripped the wheel, ready to hit the road at a moment's notice. North, as usual, glanced around, checking for threats from behind before he climbed into the vehicle.

"Target's dead, Matthew, but take the long route back to the loft. I want to build some extra distance as a precaution, you know, just in case."

Matthew smiled in delight, knowing North's strategy had worked like a charm despite all the risks. "Roger that, boss," he said, respecting his accomplishments as he ignited the engine and drove off.

North laid back in his seat as they drove away, grinning from ear to ear. He had pulled off the impossible for the second time in nearly seventeen hours. He had walked into a public building of thousands and eliminated another member of Her Majesty's government without anyone noticing. It was a feat that made him feel alive, like a legend no one could ever or would touch.

Chapter 15

Ripley spent the entire journey to the Section soothing her rage. She'd given herself two full minutes to feel sorry for not stopping North. As a result, she vented her anger out on some poor sod's vehicle, essentially breaking his rear tail light. She left a number to cover the damage when she refocused, knowing there was no point in losing herself over him. He wasn't worth it, in any way, shape, or form. Besides, feeling like shit wouldn't do anyone any good, least of all those North had already murdered in pursuit of trying to stop him today.

Upon arriving, the bomb crews had finished disabling the explosive with next to no issues. It may have looked terrifying with all the Semtex stacked up inside, but for them, it was nothing. It's a daily occurrence. They just took it in their stride, moving on to the next threat. For Ripley, though, it was a far different scenario. They may have prevented the carnage of North murdering hundreds of innocent bystanders, but they were still no closer to finding him. North was using his knowledge of the agency's protocols to stay hidden, leaving them a fake bread trail to follow so that he could hunt these MPs of his without a single notion of concern for his well-being. It meant they've been at a disadvantage from the start, playing constant catch-up while he roamed around murdering as he pleased. Still, amid all the chaos, the carnage he'd produced, they gained an insight into his operation, courtesy of his driver.

He hadn't spoken a word since being taken away. The discovery of the explosive was more of a shock to him than to anyone else. Ripley figured it was due to him being in the dark about the contents of the package, but that didn't make him clean, not in her eyes. He still volunteered to play his role in North's scheme, helping set up all this mayhem she'd witnessed. So, his hands would remain stained in this just as much as North's were, whether he cared to admit it or not.

Ripley had the driver placed into the interrogation room below the Section as she headed upstairs. She figured it would help to lose his tongue as she left him alone, chained to the desk inside, with nothing but his misdeeds to stew over.

Upon re-entry, the Section was far busier than ever. In light of the extreme nature of the threat posed by North, Denver had called for all hands-on deck. As a result, the rest of their support staff arrived to assist with the matter. Their primary roles were to comb through all intel received, handle incoming traffic, and review every other piece of data they collected. Aside from that, they assisted all senior staff like herself and Harper in running the daily operations.

Ripley was en route to check in with Harper; however, she found him buried in papers once she reached his desk. He was still busy allocating assignments to various staff members to help map out the potential escape routes surrounding the finance centre North could have taken. Ripley decided it was best to leave him for a minute as he listed street names after street names for the staff to scrutinise over. Instead, she opted to debrief with the chief.

Upon approaching his office, Denver sat at his desk in what looked like a heated phone call discussion based on the vibe of his body language and tone.

"Sir, with respect, we are doing whatever we can to stop these killings from happening, and as soon as we have an update on the situation, we will inform you of it right away. Now, if you please, excuse me, I have a section to run," Denver said, slamming the receiver down.

He sat, wondering if that was the right way or not to end the call before simply brushing it off. Despite their shortcomings, the Section was still the most promising chance at apprehending North, and they knew it, despite their apprehension.

"Let me guess, number ten?" Ripley said, leaning against the frame.

Denver turned, facing her with a sense of annoyance. "They're displeased with our current efforts in stopping North."

Ripley scrunched her nose at the government's appraisal of the situation. She saw how quick they were to criticise their actions as they sat behind their desks, taking zero risks, in stopping this madness themselves.

"You'd think they'd be a tad grateful. I mean, we just stopped a massive explosion going off in London, saving who knows how many lives from a horrific end."

"Alas, they don't see it that way. Based on what I gather, the death of Miss Lee has them all scared shitless, afraid of who may be the next one to join her in the morgue. They're trying to keep it quiet, of course, to help reduce the sense of panic among the MPs and maintain control, but it won't last. Press is already getting wind of the bomb threat, so it won't take long before they all hear about North's latest victim."

Ripley looked away in disdain, knowing their sentiment rang true. They've been blind to who North's been targeting all day. He'd carried out this rampage, setting up all these explosive traps, murdering MPs without a shred of a worry about being discovered. It left her with a sickening taste, knowing it was all happening under her watch, and she'd done nothing to prevent it. After all, it was her job to do so.

As Denver watched, he noticed the contempt on her face, theorising the events of the previous few hours were playing on her more than she cared to let on. "What of our guest? Any word from him?" Denver asked, trying to entice her into discussing the work, keeping her distracted from the self-doubt plaguing her mind.

"Not yet. The driver's scared though, trying to hide it, acting like a tough bloke," she remarked, locking her sights back on him. "But I've seen the fear in his eyes. Play this right; he'll tell us what he knows about North. I can almost guarantee it."

Denver smirked in response, detecting the fire still burning in her voice. The virtue she needed to keep pushing, despite the guilt she felt ridden with over what had transpired today.

"Good, very good. Oh, and, I almost forgot, excellent work averting that explosive."

"Thanks, chief," she said as a brief smile appeared across her face as Denver stood with pride, approaching her.

"I mean it. Despite how this appears, we've removed North's distraction thanks to your efforts. We've also gained an insight into the vehicle he's using and even have his accomplice in chains one floor below us. Who's the closest lead we've had all day in locating this bastard, and we owe that to you and you alone."

Ripley gazed at Denver, unsure of what to say. His short words of praise had revitalised the fight in her, knowing that they were still in this, that North hadn't won, not yet, anyway.

Denver was pleased to see her strength return. His true intention was to remind her that each success they've achieved today was because of her efforts and nothing more. Still, he realised that no matter how much he trusted her to be the right person to stop this chaos, he couldn't gamble everything on it.

"Like I said earlier, I trust your judgment. Whatever it takes, find out what you can from our guest. I'll do the same with my inquiries."

"I will, but where are you sneaking off to?"

"North's a contract killer. He isn't doing this because a few MPs have wronged him. Someone's hired him to carry out their kill list. It's probably the same person feeding him their itineraries. It's a long shot, but I have an off-book project that might be useful in this matter."

Ripley nodded, leaning off the frame with a renewed sense of optimism that they were still in the fight. They could still find North and prevent further innocent individuals from being murdered by him today.

The pair exited his office. Ripley headed straight towards Harper, who was now by himself, while Denver departed on his mission to end this mayhem. She hovered over his shoulder as he finished his latest call regarding street address before leaning into his gaze once he placed the receiver down.

"Did you find anything out about our mystery guest?"

Harper cracked a grin as he shook his head in dismay at her. "My dear, did you seriously think I wouldn't find anything out for you?" he replied, yanking a file out from a large stack in his tray and dropping it into her hands.

"You are nothing but a silent marvel. You know that, right?"

Harper leaned back, looking most modestly at her. "Oh, I know. I only hope it can help, as I'm having zero luck tracking North's vehicle or even him. My guess is he's sticking to the back routes to avoid detection, so unless we know his reg or the bloody street he left from, the search won't become any easier as we widen the radius."

"Doesn't surprise me. North's been off the grid for almost eight years and was better at counter-surveillance than most agents," she remarked. After that, she flipped through the file, glancing through their guest's history, studying every aspect of his life as a serviceman.

"But the good news is that the explosive may provide us with another lead. According to the bomb unit, the explosive was to be triggered by a mobile messaging system."

"What, like a text?"

"Yep, no doubt the only person with that number is North. Luckily I've set up a net, so if he messages that number at all, it will appear to him it's activated, and I'll be able to pin his exact location within seconds."

Ripley smirked at his scheme, confident that with all the different angles the Section was now navigating with, one of their moves would lead them to the man himself. She glanced over at the report, flipping through another couple of pages. She then re-scanned over all the details of the driver's career, and life, until she came across what she needed.

"I reckon this can work for me, Alife. Thank you," she said, heading downstairs to chat with their mystery guest.

Chapter 16

Ripley burst into the interrogation room, causing the driver to startle in his seat as she slammed the door shut behind her. Ripley wanted him scared, and from the sweat dripping off his face, he seemed on the tipping point of cracking. All it would take was the right amount of pressure to persuade him to talk.

Ripley sat in front of him, realising she had lost count of all the times she'd been in a room like this one. They always seemed to have the same plain grey stone walls or panels. It was as if everyone bought them all from the same wholesale supplier when they were building interrogation rooms. It also included a package deal on custom light fixtures that help create a gloomy setting, specifically designed to keep prisoners in a constant state of fear without any other practical uses.

Afraid of what was about to happen, the driver slumped into his seat, avoiding eye contact with Ripley, remaining silent as he stared down at his chains. Ripley, meanwhile, lay there, watching the lone figure, sensing the fear oozing off him. She assessed that physical pain wouldn't have the right effect, potentially throwing him into shock, causing him to clam up, and rendering him useless. It meant she'd have to employ a different approach to get him to open up.

Ripley tossed his file onto the table, dividing them, leaning back in silence, smiling, waiting for him to react. After a full sixty seconds of continuous staring had elapsed, it was clear that he wasn't planning to say anything. Still, she could tell that he was becoming more and more agitated by her presence as her eyes burned away in his mind. It made him feel extremely uncomfortable, as he kept staring at his chains, not knowing where else to look. After a few more seconds, she decided it was time to apply the emotional pressure to break those cracks.

"Your name's Steve Crick, twenty-one years old, with five of those spent in the fifth Northumberland Fusiliers' regiment in Syria before returning home fourteen weeks ago."

Steve glanced up at Ripley for the first time since she sat down. He knew she was trying to play him by spelling out his entire life story, thinking she knew about him, his past, the person he was, but she didn't. She was just his jailer, nothing more.

"Lawyer, I'm not saying anything until I speak to one," he said, trying to hide his worry as much as he could, remembering he still had rights.

Ripley laughed at his remark, thinking he could make any demands as she leaned forward.

"No, that's not how this will work, prick." Steve was about to open his mouth to respond, but Ripley swiftly raised her palm to his face for him to stop. She then lost any notion of her laughter. "No, you're not talking now. You're going to sit there and listen, and if you decide to interrupt me again, you'll lose some teeth, you hear?"

Steve stared at Ripley's display of aggression and reluctantly nodded to please her. Still, it did nothing to soothe the growing anxiety he was trying to bury. For each second of silence that elapsed, he became more and more frightened of his well-being, not knowing what to expect.

"David North," she said, lowering her palm and voice to avoid confusion over what she wanted. "You're going to tell me where to find him. Otherwise, we'll happily pin every death on you and you alone since last night."

Steve looked back, confused, wondering what she was referring to, while Ripley remained nothing but indifferent.

"Now, you may think that wasn't me. I'm just a driver in all this, but know that if we cannot find North, they will hold someone accountable for this. And trust me, after discovering what you were driving about with, no one in this government will lose any sleep watching you rot away in a cell until the end of days."

Steve was about to respond to her absurdity but resisted the urge for fear of retaliation. He still felt the irritation in the back of his knee from where she struck him. The discomfort caused him to sweat more, dreading what she might decide to do to him. He wiped the top of his head with his shoulder as best he could before straightening up and facing Ripley. He had nothing but hate in his eyes for what she was suggesting as he vowed to remain steadfast, like the brave soldier he was.

Ripley remained unfazed by the situation, extending her arm to pull the report back. "Speak then. Where is North?"

Steve stared back, not uttering a single syllable at her request, but Ripley could see the increased moisture dripping off him onto his chains. She guessed he was trying to play smart, not saying anything, waiting for a lawyer or some official to arrive. Then he could cut a deal, escape punishment and continue being a free man, like so many others before him.

Still, that wasn't happening here. As far as Ripley saw it, anyone associated with North in this was equally responsible for every death that occurred today. This was especially true of those from the warehouse she'd witnessed screaming out in agony for the flames to stop, for their suffering to end. Ripley knew what type of pressure it would take to crack him open. It meant crossing a line others wouldn't dare, but they weren't in her boots, facing the threat she was, with the number of innocents already lost. With that in mind, Ripley opened the file, reading the details over one last time before opening her mouth. She might have regretted what she was about to say but didn't let it alter her voice, not one decibel.

"I see your mother still lives alone in Wyndham Tower since your father's passing."

Frozen with shock, Steve could only stare into Ripley's eyes. He repeated what she said over and over in his mind, trying to imagine it was a misunderstanding, that he didn't just hear what she'd said. Ripley, however, just tilted her head back, fixing her sights on Steve's gaze, showing no shame, no sign of regret, but confident that she'd hit a nerve.

"Flat 191. I wonder how her neighbours will react, knowing she raised a murderer like you. I figure they'll show their appreciation for her raising such a stand-up citizen. If not, well, I can easily teach them how.

Steve was fully aware of Ripley's intention to ruin his mother's livelihood. It's messed up even to consider such a thing, let alone use it in practice. When fighting on the front lines, he knew all about respecting the enemy, ensuring the conflict remained between them and no one else. You wouldn't dare touch people like the parents who played no part in their child's crime. He prayed she wouldn't act on it and that it was just an empty threat as he examined her, searching for a sense of humanity, but there wasn't any. Her green eyes were as cold as ice, without a flicker of sympathy in sight.

"You're sick for even suggesting that, you fucking bitch!"

Ripley didn't flinch at his remark, having heard a lot worse from more menacing individuals in her time. She instead closed the report, leaning forward towards him, not giving a damn what his opinion of her was. Lives were on the line, innocent individuals who didn't deserve to be butchered by some psychopath. She would do whatever it took to ensure that such a thing wouldn't happen again.

"Everything you know about North and his plan. That's the price to ensure your mother doesn't pay, in her blood, for your crimes."

Steve sat in silence, struggling to comprehend how to deal with such a horrible situation for his mother. Pictures of her getting beaten, terrorised and rushed out of her home because of his mistake filtered through his mind on repeat. Each time he watched them, he became more and more horrified, powerless to stop them.

Ripley, meanwhile, kept her gaze, seeing he was teetering at the edge, as he slumped further into the chair, calculating he needed one final push.

"Remember, North never told you about his bomb. He's willing to murder you for his plan to succeed, but think about this: if North escapes our grasp, he'll want his revenge for you getting peckish and losing his bomb."

Steve sank deeper into the chair. His heart pounded heavier than it ever had. Even when he was in combat, with a shower of bullets fired at him, it was nowhere near this loud because she was right. A man like North would never understand his pathetic excuse for being hungry. He'd messed up the primary job he had to do for him, no doubt about it. It was something he would never forget about. He'd come for him. Whatever it took, North would seek vengeance for his stupid blunder, killing him like any of the countless targets he'd ever hunted.

Ripley watched him squirm in his chair, knowing he was so close to spilling his guts as she gave him one last thrust.

"North doesn't care if you live or die. It's a fact. So talk to me and survive this because you owe him nothing."

Steve turned away, absorbing everything, replaying it all over in his mind before opening his mouth. He realised he might be a dead man walking, but he still had a duty of care to protect his mother, more than anyone else, from this madness.

"I . . . I don't know what he intends to do. He kept that hidden from us. All North hired me to do was buy him some clothes and drive that Volvo around. Honestly, that's all I ever did for him. Nothing connected to the bomb or these killings," he said, praying she would believe him.

Ripley leaned back, somewhat disappointed, but concluded someone like North wouldn't explain anything sufficient to Steve, being just a grunt in his master plan.

"What sort of clothes?" she asked, wondering what else he knew.

"Some overalls, and pieces of a suit."

"What type of suit?"

"Nothing special, just whatever was on sale in the store."

"Alright, what was he intending to use them for?"

"I don't know, as I said, North kept us in the dark regarding his plans."

Ripley was about to ask another question but stopped before the words left her mouth. She registered something of significance, he said and wondered how she had missed it the first time.

"What do you mean by us?"

"Umm, North, he has another guy with him, Matthew. I think that's who he was. I never caught his surname."

Ripley leaned forward, believing that it was just the two of them. It had never occurred to her to consider a third individual involved in all of this. It meant there was now another potential link to locate North.

"Do you know where he might be?"

Steve glanced into the air, trying to think before responding. "I mean, he might be back at the loft. It's where I met them both this morning."

"This loft, where is it?" Ripley demanded.

Steve stared into the air, thinking of the address before it sprang to mind. "Asylum church, no chapel, Asylum Chapel. It's in Peckham."

Ripley nodded back. She had her lead on North, albeit slim, but was thankful to have it.

"I'll see to your mum's safety. You have my word," she said, stepping away and exiting the room.

With all his strength, Steve clasped his head, crying with relief, knowing he wouldn't have his mother suffer in pain for his own stupid mistakes. However, he tried not to dwell on what would happen to her if North were to escape and come searching for his revenge. In any case, he may decide to inflict it on the one person who bought him into this world as a just trade for his betrayal.

Ripley walked down the corridor, pulled out her mobile and dialled upstairs.

"Harper, I have a probable location on North. I'm sending it to you now. Once you have it, contact CTSFO to have a team meet me there. I'll need support to apprehend North if he's still on site."

Chapter 17

North smiled with excitement as he re-entered the loft, feeling like a champion. The second target was dead, and his plan worked like a charm. Thanks to his bomb threat, the security forces were virtually blind to his actions. He re-approached his table, starting the last stages of prep for the upcoming target. Due to time constraints, his employer needed them dead within the next few hours. He, therefore, left Matthew to check in on Steve to ensure he wasn't getting antsy after sitting in a car for hours, listening to whatever songs the radio chose to play on repeat.

North placed his rucksack on the floor and sat down, yanking his laptop out. He opened it up and logged into his email account. The entire page was blank, with no messages in the inbox. The only thing that stood out was a single saved message in the drafts folder. Upon seeing it, North smiled and double-clicked it. It took much longer than he liked, but his employer had finally come through with all the info on the last target, Anil Singh. Still, it didn't change his displeasure at how the information came in, bit by bit, being against his preferred way of operating. He'd always requested everything from the client on the target once he accepted a job, ensuring he always gave himself enough prep time to carry out the kill.

He, however, overlooked it here since the employer was an old comrade of his who had provided him with plenty of high-paid jobs in the past. Due to this, he had to operate more gun and run instead of his preferred clean precision style. Still, the fee he was to collect afterwards made all the changes worthwhile.

For this reason, he created this private email account for him years ago. It was so the two could easily pass on their messages without the fear of being caught since no one had invented the means to trace an unsent email.

In spite of his employer's lateness, he couldn't discount his ability to gather the right amount of information. As usual, he had everything he wanted on the target, addresses, an itinerary for the entire afternoon, the vehicle he was driving, and even the layout of his office. The only thing left was to determine where to execute him. He opened up his search engines, exploring the various areas around the locations Singh would be visiting. He scanned every line of detail on the page, evaluating the most optimal place where he could intercept and eliminate him. Next, he assessed the most effective method to use. Like his colleagues, he considered sneaking into Singh's office to blow his brains out. Still, given the limited time left, he fancied using the rest of his explosives, rigging his vehicle to blow once he started the engine. Alternatively, he could still access a sniper through one of his connections and pick him off with a headshot once he finished for the day. Each idea floated about his mind as North imagined acting them all out. He analysed each method's flaw, the likelihood of success, and the ease of use, as he singled out the ideal one to use on Singh. He was so absorbed in his fantasy that he didn't even notice when Matthew rushed back inside.

"North, it's over," he howled.

Matthew's words broke North's concentration as he turned, facing him with a sour expression. As soon as North locked eyes with him, he seemed to be in a state of shock. It was like he had experienced a supernatural entity. His skin was turning whiter by the second.

"What's happened? Is it Steve? Did he mess up the pickup?"

"No idea. I can't reach him, but that's not the point. The bomb's online. It's online for the entire fucking world to see."

North didn't respond right away, as he sat frozen, utterly bewildered, as Matthew approached.

"What do you mean?" he asked, concealing his concern.

"News reports. There's been a bomb scare in west London. This can't be a coincidence. It must be yours. We're done," Matthew said, shoving the news article from his mobile into his face.

North snatched it in utter disbelief, thinking it couldn't be true. He couldn't have lost his advantage; there was no way. He'd read the report thrice before tossing it back, opening up new search engines on his laptop to see if the same results came up. Sure enough, they did. North read each of the reports, line by line, to ensure he didn't miss any details, keeping his composure throughout. Unfortunately, though, they all repeated the same piece of information relating to Shepherd's Bush market being closed for the same reason. He considered reaching into his pocket to trigger the bomb, thinking it may be fake, a plan to lure him out. However, he stopped before grabbing it, believing they were waiting for him to click it to zero in on his location.

Instead, North sat, tapping his fingers away on the keypad, thinking the entire situation over. He'd lost his distraction. *Somehow.* Somehow, they found it faster than he ever expected. He questioned himself over and over again in his mind, realising he'd missed something. He couldn't explain it any other way. There was a flaw in his master plan, one he didn't see, and because of it, everything else was in peril. It didn't sit right, not knowing how to process something like this. Unlike anything North could ever remember, he was at an actual disadvantage, and his stomach was in knots over it.

North hid his self-resentment well from Matthew, wanting to maintain his dominance. He knew if he saw him distressed, he'd start losing his self-control and start panicking, resulting in nothing but mistakes. It was something he couldn't afford now, not with the security services' attention no longer split. It wouldn't take long to find them, not with their resources. They were slow in his eyes but not stupid. However, in his moment of self-doubt and resentment, North couldn't help but consider the silver lining of having the details for the last target.

He knew they were unaware of his employer. All the information they've ever exchanged was via the draft method that no one could track. There was no doubting the authenticity of the info either, given that his old friend had more to lose if all three targets weren't dead come morning. No deal could save his future, only their deaths.

His luck had held out for so many years through various horrendous situations, and he'd survived them all. He realised that if he was to play it right, he could still complete the job and disappear with his money, just as he had intended. With such a move, his reputation would only reach new heights. The fees he could charge in the future would be enormous if he were to complete what he could refer to as the impossible job. Perhaps it would be enough for him to retire before his body finally broke, and he could no longer hunt targets as he did in his younger days.

He turned away from the screen, pondering this opportunity once more, before turning to Matthew, who'd finally regained the colour on his face.

"We're not running. I have the itinerary for the last target, so we're carrying on and finishing this job," North announced without a shred of worry.

Matthew stared at him, unable to comprehend how North could want to continue in such dire circumstances.

"You told me the bomb was your advantage, designed to divert the security services' attention so that they wouldn't find us. Without it, I'm sorry — but how are we not screwed?" Matthew asked, trying to reason with him.

North just stared back, rebuilding his self-belief. He reflected upon the hundreds of missions he had carried out in Iraq before becoming an agency hitman to a freelance assassin. Across all those years, he never once hesitated to take on any task or contract that came his way. No matter how suicidal or impossible they seemed, he consistently achieved the kill. He never gave up, no matter what. It's why his clients loved him so much. North could accomplish the most hazardous assignments that no one else had the balls to take on, despite how much money they would offer.

His brutality had earned him the nickname of being the most vicious killer to come out of England. It was a title North was prouder to wear compared to any of the senseless pats on the back his bosses in the agency occasionally bestowed on him. It made him feel alive, like a living legend no one could touch. However, everything he'd achieved, all of it, would forever remain tainted if he ran away. It would be the mark of a coward. It would ruin him, dismantle the name he'd built for so long. Still, he wasn't about to let that happen, not now, not over something like this. He was too talented for that.

North stood in front of Matthew, towering over him with his presence, who dropped his head in fear of what repercussions North might have for questioning him. Instead, he just placed one hand on his shoulder, gently lifting his head.

"They've been lucky with the bomb, nothing more, but my true advantage is they have zero clue who I'm targeting. We still possess the upper hand, so we're finishing this job, together."

Matthew stared, knowing how deranged it sounded, but he was right. First, there are hundreds of registered MPs, and the security services didn't have the resources to protect them all, not on their excuse of a budget. In addition, he'd already seen North achieve the impossible twice today. Therefore, it made sense to believe he could do it again, despite the added pressure they now faced.

North lightened up once he saw the gears turning in Matthew's mind, realising how right he was, that this still could be done. He knew Matthew would stick with him now, nervous as shit, but with him till the end. It was why he liked him. Matthew may have never been in a proper firefight, but that wasn't the point. What mattered was remaining a true loyalist who would obey and follow his orders to the letter, but not blindly, as he used to in his younger days. After those pricks who sat in offices, away from all the bloodshed that war brings, saw his talent and hired him to carry out their missions. For his part, he cleaned up their messes and assassinated their targets so that they could earn themselves a better office without getting anything in return. It was an act North did without fault for more years than he cared to recall until he finally saw sense and threw all their bullshit, their lies, behind to craft something for himself.

Although they were at different skill levels, Matthew could think for himself, and North respected that. With him guiding and nurturing his future, he knew they could accomplish wonders in contract killing. However, their mood suddenly turned as North's smile faded upon hearing the rhythmic four-beeping coming from his laptop.

The pair stood stunned as the hair on the back of their necks bristled in fear of what the dreaded sound signified, knowing what was to come.

Chapter 18

As a precaution, North had set up a motion sensor camera linked to his laptop on the outskirts of his hideout, which now detected movement. North rushed to his screen, seeing the live feed of a van along with an Audi driving past less than four seconds ago. He immediately recognised the models as the ones CTSFO used, having ridden with them in the past. They'd found him.

North hid his discomfort well, maintaining the façade of a man in control while inside, everything was falling apart. For the first and only time in a twenty-plus career, he felt a sense of self-loss, like he was no longer in control.

"This complicates things a lot. The enemy's inbound," North said with disgust, gesturing at Matthew, whose colour faded from his face once again as he stared at the screen. North felt his stomach twisting itself together for the second time today over the impending situation. He figured he had maybe three minutes before they burst into the loft at a push.

He sat in silence, contemplating the situation, considering the only two options he had to play, retreat, or engage. There was no form of surrender in this, not for him. It was never his style. Instead, he was always used to shooting his way out, a lesson he'd learned during his first tour in Iraq after squads of enemy combatants ambushed his unit.

They stood in front of the village they had defended as bullets rained down from all sides, mowing down soldiers. They attempted to return fire, but it soon became apparent, from the squeals of their friends in agony, that it was pointless to fight. Deep down, as their hearts pounded uncontrollably, the soldiers knew there was no escaping the massacre ahead. However, as they prepared for the end, North held his ground, firing back with every bullet in his rifle. He slaughtered target after target without a single bit of sympathy entering his subconscious for who they were. His talent to not die in some desert, so far away from home, by some worthless prick, as he liked to call them, kept the enemy at bay until support arrived.

Years later, in every mission he ever served or target he'd ever hunted, he never once forgot about the exhilaration of his first battle. The way he defied the odds others around him considered impossible. It gave him the confidence to know that no matter how volatile the situation may appear, he had overcome the odds once before; therefore, he could do it again with ease.

As North weighed up his options, a thought crossed his mind. It was something he should have registered sooner but found himself too frustrated by losing his advantage to examine. If they'd found the explosive, they'd have Steve, too. North realised he must've betrayed him. It was the only way they could have located him this fast, seeing as no one outside of the three of them was aware of the hideout. He believed he could rely on Steve and trust him to stand by him like Matthew, but he was mistaken. North made a mental note to find the traitor later on and drill a bullet into his brain for his betrayal. For now, though, there was a far more pressing issue North was only comprehending. If Steve told them about the hideout, what else did he reveal? The traitor may have only been around him in person for a couple of minutes in the morning, but during that time, he could have easily heard or seen something specific — *"Idiot, you idiot."*

North mumbled it to himself, ensuring Matthew didn't hear as he dropped his head in shame, tapping himself on the forehead, remembering — remembering his mistake. Steve was standing behind him when he studied the last target in the morning. He'd always done it for his targets, examining their features so he could pick them out in a crowd if required. The stupidest part was that he had headphones plugged in, listening to Singh's voice from some interview. It's why he didn't observe Steve when he should have. He'd been careless and now was suffering the consequences of it.

Steve could have spotted his face and revealed it to the security services, who would finally know who he was targeting. Anil Singh could be enroute to some random safe house in Cornwall, protected under heavy guard, safe from any of his actions during this exact moment. North knew he couldn't let that happen. Beyond everything else he was struggling with, he couldn't let Singh, the last target of his job, escape and wreck everything he'd accomplished today, not over one foolish blunder.

"Change of plan. I'm engaging them," he said, addressing Matthew without a hint of worry.

Matthew stared at him, baffled, hoping he might have just misspoken. "I'm sorry. What are you planning to do?"

North stood up, starring Matthew in the eyes, having found an element of control as he formulated his response for the inbound enemy. "We're compromised. That bastard Steve has betrayed us and revealed our location. I need to know what else he's told them; otherwise, all of this, all of it, would have been for nothing."

Matthew stood there bemused, unsure of what to think of it.

"Relax, I know their procedures. I even helped develop a few. So, I know some agent is leading these officers who'll have the exact info I want," North remarked.

Matthew continued to stare back with a mixture of shock and amazement. He'd heard the stories about North's reckless shootouts like everyone else, how he defied the odds and survived the unthinkable; however, he never believed he would be a part of it. He figured he would only stay in the car, do his driving and clean his weapons, not exchange bullets with trained professionals.

"How the hell can you do that? I've never been in a combat situation like this or even engaged a proper live target before," he said, hiding his terror over what lay ahead.

North whipped out two small packs of explosives from his rucksack, waving them in his face. "With these," he exclaimed.

Matthew stared back in horror at the thought of what would happen. He'd met enough soldiers who'd lost body parts to IEDs in his time in Syria. Most of them continued to live somewhat decent lives once they learned to make some sense of the horrors that led to their lost limbs. Still, never in his wildest fantasies did he dream of joining them, of feeling that disgusting sense they all buried deep within their stomachs once they caught sight of their disfigured self, wondering why — *Why in God's name did this happen to me?*

In contrast, North remained calm as a sea turtle, ignoring any uncertainty swimming across his mind about what he was proposing.

"Trust me. I know what I'm doing. I need you to sneak out, take all the gear and have the BM ready to move the second I step out," he said with so much certainty that Matthew didn't even try to argue.

Despite how deranged it seemed, he had unnatural faith in North. He couldn't detect a whiff of fear in the man, unsure whether it was a positive thing. Still, the confidence he exuded made him believe he'd pull it off. Somehow, he'd pull it off, like in every other dire situation he'd ever faced. Matthew, though was just thankful not to be in the room when all the explosives went off. He knew it was the only way to ensure he wouldn't end up in a body bag.

Matthew scooped up all the gear rushing out of the loft in a flash. In the meantime, North connected the explosives to a tiny trigger switch, arming them upon hearing the engine approaching outside. North calculated he had maybe fifty seconds left before they reached the loft's interior. However, there was only one way in or out to his advantage. North knew how to play it, rushing to place the explosive beside the door. He buried it away so that when they burst in, no one would notice, but close enough to cause some considerable damage. He dashed back to his table, flipping it over with his stool, hiding the explosives behind it, but then he heard it. It was the sound of the engine cutting out and the faint echo of footsteps growing louder. They'd dispersed. North estimated he had about twenty seconds left, but it didn't matter. It was all set.

He took several deep breaths, calming his growing knots, realising that what he was about to undertake was extremely dangerous, even for someone with his talents. Still, he didn't see a way around it. He needed to know what Steve saw. If he'd witnessed Singh's face and revealed it to the security services, it would ruin him, destroy the name he worked so hard to cultivate, all over one stupid self-made error. It was something he was adamant not to let happen. Whatever the cost, he would remedy this mistake.

North stepped back, positioning himself at the correct distance from the explosives, ensuring that he wouldn't lose any of his limbs if it turned out wrong. Next, he yanked out his mobile, pressing it against his ear while arming the switch in his opposite palm. He hid it within his sleeves so no one would notice but easy enough to trigger with a single click once the moment arose.

The sound of the officers smashing into the door echoed throughout the building. They were inside. It was time, so he belted into his mobile at the top of his lungs, pacing around, deep into an imaginary argument.

"No. No, you will not mess with my money, do you hear? I don't give a damn what problems you're having. You will transfer what you owe me now. No — not in an hour, shithead, now!"

North listened as their footsteps grew louder, closing in on his position. He, therefore, kept up his pretence, ensuring the officers would believe that he wasn't faking, but on a legitimate call.

"You still want these MPs dead? Do you? This is what it will take, and you will pay. Do you understand? You'll stop stalling and pay!"

The officers stormed into the room after his last word, SIG716 rifles trained on him, completely unaware of the horror surrounding them, as they inched forward towards their target.

North twisted around, selling his genuine shock for all he could, making it look as natural as possible to avoid any awkward glances.

"Shitting — hell," he said aloud in the correct shocked tone.

"Don't move. Show us your hands, now!" The commander barked.

North remained calm but let them know he was stunned beyond words. He cautiously raised his arms, ensuring they thought they'd caught him with his dick in his hand. He knew they would expect him to set some trap after his taster this morning and knew he couldn't fool with anything so extreme. He only had a few seconds to plan his response, but this was it. The only solution he could come up with was to keep their attention focused on him and avoid wandering eyes that might notice his explosives. Even if it only lasted for a handful of seconds, it was all he needed to get them inside the blast radius without being ripped to shreds by bullets, believing their red-blooded nature would stay dominant. Instead, they would remain the professional they were and take him in alive, if only to know who the mysterious person at the end of his imagery call was.

"Drop the phone!" the commander barked.

North stood still as his mobile hit the ground, watching the commander inch closer to him. Her officers flanked from the sides, fixing sights on him, searching for the slightest hint of a threat to fire at.

"Knees now! Put your hands behind your head."

North sank to his knees, steadying his hands behind him. He had no intention of encouraging the officers to shoot at him as they edged their irrevocable steps into his trap. He instead followed their requests to the letter, giving them the sense of control they desired. Once the commander took her last few steps forward to apprehend him, North noticed the oddball within the group. It wasn't difficult, considering she was the only one not in full combat gear. He figured this young redhead was likely the agent who would have the answers he craved.

He watched her as she shuffled into the room. As she closed in behind the officers, he could have sworn she was about to say something. Perhaps it was to warn them or something along those lines, that she'd felt his trap and knew what he was doing. Still, it was too late.

The commander extended her hand out to seize North; however, the second her fingers touched his sleeve, he took it as his moment, striking the trigger against the back of his neck.

Every person had the same instant sense of horror and disbelief as soon as they heard the roar of the explosions in their eardrums. The blinding light of both blasts followed it in rapid succession, sending everyone plummeting to the ground except for those unfortunate officers closest to the bombs. Their bodies ended up mutilated beyond all recognition, even by those who loved them most. Meanwhile, aware of what was coming, North leapt back, snatching hold of the commander in front of him. Then, using her as a human shield, he dragged her down to defend himself from the blast.

The horrific act ended in the mere blink of an eye as the dust produced from the explosions settled across the room. The officers all lay on the ground, unconscious but in various states of pain. Some of them had missing limbs, others had pieces of shrapnel stuck inside, but all were bleeding out to death. Over eighty seconds of nothing but pure, unfiltered silence passed before North tossed the bleeding commander off. Then, after pocketing his mobile, he forced himself up, coughing over the smoke filling his lungs but smiling. He glanced over his work with sheer pride in himself for having again defied the odds. He had eliminated an entire CTSFO team single-handedly and lived to tell the tale, a feat no one else could ever claim.

His body was still shaking from the blast, but he stepped forward, pulling out his pistol. Meanwhile, everyone else lay on the floor, unconscious and unaware of what happened, as North hobbled over their bodies towards his prize. He stood over her body, gazing down, examining it. There were no visible signs of shrapnel sticking out of her flesh, a few cuts across the torso, but nothing fatal. Despite the horrors, she seemed to have been extremely lucky to survive. North bent down, checking her pulse, chuckling as he felt it beat steadily. She was alive, for now. Then, with all his remaining strength, he lifted her over his shoulder, hobbling his way out of the loft.

Once North reached outside, he'd spotted Matthew, who'd successfully made it out, following his command to the letter, sitting in the vehicle, ready to drive off. His eyes fixed on the rearview mirror, clutching his Glock, staring, waiting to determine who or if anyone would exit the building. As soon as he saw North emerge, he was beaming. After seeing the team that charged in, he could hardly believe it, but there he stood, David North, the living legend, with his prize.

"Open the boot," North barked, trying to cough out the last of the dust trapped in his lungs, and like the loyalist he was, Matthew rushed out, obeying his command.

They shoved the agent inside before binding her hands with the cable ties in her vest after they tore it off. North didn't want to take any chances of her fighting back, regardless of her state. He continued fishing into her pockets, patting her down as he tossed her wallet away, smashing her mobile on the ground. Then, after finding her ID card, North flipped it open, discovering her name was Naomi Ripley. A smug grin crossed his face as he gaped over her battered body before pocketing the card and slamming the boot down, sealing his prize inside.

Chapter 19

Denver laid back against a bench in St. James Park, watching the people going about their typical day. Kids were playing around on the swing set. Joggers zipped past on their daily runs. People were stopping to admire and take snaps of the palace, while others were overfeeding the ducks, as usual. It was quite a pleasant day to be out and about with the sun shining down. Denver figured maybe in a couple of years, when he reached that rare thing they called retirement in this job, he could enjoy a day like this. Then, free from all the stress of agency life, he could buy a beagle and take it out for long walks in the park, enjoying the simplicity of everyday life. However, that wasn't today though. He was still section chief and had a job to prevent further slaughter from yet another madman.

At that point, a woman sat down on the bench next to him. She was pretty young compared to Denver but dressed in the same smart business attire he wore. Neither of them looked at each other as the woman scanned the crowd, wondering if anyone had noticed her.

"You can relax. The assassin isn't interested in murdering the home secretary's assistant," Denver said, trying to ease her growing nerves as he faced her. After a few moments, it seemed as if the effect had worked, as the woman breathed a sigh of relief, settling onto the bench. As she watched, the ducks in front bobbled their heads back and forth across the water, enthralled by each other's company.

"In case I forget to mention it later, thank you, Mrs Wilson, for meeting me under such unusual circumstances, but I believe you can help with my investigation for your boss's murderer."

Mrs Wilson peeked at him, worried about what he'd said. "So the rumours are true then. You're not even close to catching this person, are you?"

She was right, of course, the Section had no active leads. Denver hoped Ripley would turn up something with North's accomplice but couldn't gamble everything on it. He needed an alternative to prevent further carnage, and this, for better or for worse, was that solution.

"I'm afraid not. The assassin behind this is a seasoned professional. I should know; he was one of ours many years ago," he stated, masking his disdain for North.

Mrs Wilson gazed at him in shock, thinking that one of their own, an Englishman, was to blame for all this havoc. "Christ, none of them is safe then."

Denver moved closer to her, readying himself for what he had to ask of her. "I require your help. These deaths aren't random. The assassin is carrying out a kill order someone has given him."

"What do you mean, kill order?"

"For this to end, we need to find the person who employed the assassin. Otherwise, they'll continue hiring murderers like him until everyone they want is dead."

Mrs Wilson stared at him, more confused than before, agreeing to meet. She didn't know what he meant by hired assassins. All she did was take care of the secretary's schedule, get him to meetings on time, pour his coffee, and answer his phone. Nothing stood out as noteworthy or inspiring to know about professional assassins. She wasn't even at the convention when the tragedy took place, having stayed home to supervise his business in the capital.

"So, why have you come to me, then?"

Denver kept composed, knowing what he was about to say would be painful for her to hear, but he didn't have any other way of putting it.

"It's because you've been sharing his bed, unofficially, of course. So, I figured you, of all people, might hold out on certain pieces of information to avoid anything about your affair coming to light and having your husband find out," he remarked.

Horrified by what he accused her of, Mrs Wilson lashed out at him in a blind rage, striking him in the shoulder with what strength she had.

"You asshole, how dare you to accuse me of such a thing when you've asked me for my help!" she protested.

Denver, though, did not respond. He instead remained silent, waiting a moment to let the shock of it all wash over.

After a handful of aimless strikes, she finally gave up, looking away from him in disgust at what he'd done, but most of all, for what he said. After that, the pair just sat on the bench in pure silence, watching the ducks in front ingest the last crumbs of bread some kids had tossed at them. The rage slowly subsided within Mrs Wilson with each one of their bites. However, the feeling soon gave way to one of dread when she awkwardly turned to Denver, wondering how he'd found out and, perhaps more importantly, who else now knew.

"How . . . how do you know?" she asked, swallowing the bulging lump in her throat.

"I run a spy agency, Mrs Wilson, so I keep an ear out for things like this if they ever need to be used in special circumstances. However, you can rest assured, that nothing will ever leak back to your husband."

Mrs Wilson looked at him with contempt over how he'd been invading her privacy, taking a minute to absorb the entire thing. But, despite how angry she felt, she knew there was no point in trying to lie, not anymore, and not to him, of all people. The secret she'd feared for so long was out.

"I . . . I, have your word on it?"

Denver nodded in response. He didn't care that she was cheating on her husband. What people do in their private lives is a matter of their own choice and theirs alone. All he wanted was to know what she was holding back on, given the current crisis. It's all he ever cared for when he had these awkward conversations with those who would prefer to protect their private affairs at the expense of those around them. Due to this, he always kept a watchful eye over specific individuals' personal lives, government officials and military personnel in most cases, but only from a distance. He never interfered with their choice or passed judgment if they wanted to be with someone who wasn't their respected partner. For whatever reasons, they told themselves to believe it was okay. Still, he knew he'd have these conversations when the situation called for it, but always with a clear conscience. He knew that the destruction of one individual's private life would never compare to those lives that faced immediate annihilation from whatever threat they faced.

Mrs Wilson took a deep breath, looking away in shame from Denver, not having the heart to face him. "There was an incident last Sunday at the Oxfam charity ball, *James*; he had a . . . a heated debate with someone I didn't recognise."

Denver hid his displeasure at her reluctance to discuss something so crucial after all that had happened, the lives lost, and those still at risk. Still, he didn't raise his voice since he knew it wouldn't help the situation. He instead maintained his calm demeanour, keeping her at ease so she felt comfortable enough to continue.

"What was it about?"

"I don't know the specifics, but, all James . . . all he said afterwards was that it was just an old dead weight MP he and his friends were planning on phasing out soon."

Denver did his utmost to hide his disappointment over what he heard, knowing she didn't disclose this information earlier. "I don't mean to pry. I never usually do, but just for my understanding, may I ask why you kept this, of all things, hidden?"

Mrs Wilsons wiped the tears from her eyes, unable to conceal the humiliation she felt over talking about her messy affair for the first time, let alone to someone she didn't know. Then, following a brief pause, gathering whatever strength she had left, she turned to him.

On seeing how distressed she had become, Denver reached out his palm to comfort her. It was something she grabbed hold of in an instant, in her desperate search for something to hold on to, when everything felt like it was slipping away from her.

"Because it all occurred outside our hotel room, James thought it would be a good night to have some fun and booked a room. However, this person somehow discovered where he was staying. He hammered on the door when we were alone, demanding to speak to him, but the person never saw me. James made me hide in the bathroom while he stepped outside to drive him away. It's why I wasn't at the convention. He didn't want to take another risk of being found out, so he made me stay behind."

She stopped to rub her burning red eyes, wiping the tears away. She realised that the embarrassment the secretary felt over being caught in the act with a married woman had saved her life. If she had been there, in his bed, last night as intended, the assassin would've gunned her down without a second thought, as he did to her lover. She knew one day she would have to confront such a disturbing thing. In essence, the humiliation her boss felt over being found out in public with her, ruining the career he'd crafted for himself, was the sole reason for her being alive right now, nothing more.

Denver stroked his hand across her back, keeping her at ease, allowing her to take a moment, to find some courage to say what she needed. She felt a great deal of regret for what she'd done, but more so for what she hadn't done.

"I'm sorry. I know I should have told someone, but the thought of it leaking out petrified me. It's the sort of story the tabloids would happily pay through their noses to publish. My, James', and my husband's innocent faces would be plastered all over the front pages forever. It's my fault, and I apologise, but I didn't know what to say. On top of everything I've done to him, I couldn't humiliate him in front of the entire world. He's a teacher, you see, and he doesn't deserve to be mocked and degraded by his students over my mess. He doesn't deserve that, or any of this, least of all me," she cried, burying her face into her sleeve, struggling to hold herself together.

Denver yanked out his handkerchief, handing it to her. She snatched it away at once, wiping away her growing tears. "Thank you for your honesty now. I promise your secret is safe with me."

It was clear to him that the utter shame she felt over her misdeeds was enough of a punishment for her to endure.

"Thank you," she said, wiping her tears. "Thank you."

After some time, Denver got up and walked away, leaving Mrs Wilson to compose herself before figuring out what she would do with her marriage. He exited the park, heading towards his vehicle, but stopped as his mobile started buzzing away in his pocket. He drew it out, seeing the red flash from the Section.

"Harper, what do you have for me?" he asked, taking the call. As he listened though, he realized the situation with North had taken a much darker turn than he could have ever imagined.

"I'm coming back now, but in the meantime, prioritise finding out everything you can about the Oxfam charity ball last Sunday. Unless I'm mistaken, whoever hired North will be there arguing with the secretary. Find that person. It may be our only link to saving Ripley.

Chapter 20

It was unclear how much time had passed following the explosion to being imprisoned inside the boot. However, the only thing Ripley knew for sure was she was on her own. Cut off from the Section, she had to find a way out of her predicament, but to her detriment, the boot she found herself in was extremely tight-spaced. North had pressed her face against the edge, meaning all she could see was darkness. She tried to wiggle about, getting a sense of the place, except her body was still reeling after the blast. Her muscles ached like mad, and being stuck in the awkward position wasn't helping. In addition, she could sense her hands tethered behind her but didn't have the strength to break them apart.

Ripley had no choice but to accept her predicament. The only thing she could do was rest and prepare herself for what was to come. Minutes of bumpy driving passed before she felt the vehicle slowing ahead of its abrupt stop. Seconds later, she heard faint voices outside, as if someone was arguing. It was difficult to tell what any of them were saying, as there was still a slight ringing in her ears.

Still, it didn't matter as the boot burst open without warning. Sunlight hit Ripley for the first time in what felt like hours before being yanked out and forced to stand. She struggled to stay straight due to her legs feeling like jelly and had to lean on the vehicle to stop herself from tumbling over.

Ripley's vision was still adjusting to the brightness, but she could still make out North in front of her. All she wanted to do was rush over and smash his face apart, breaking it into a million different tiny pieces. It was a way to honour everyone she had witnessed murder today, whose cries still echoed through her mind. However, she realised it wasn't possible in her current state, so she buried the idea. She knew she needed to play smart. North took her captive instead of murdering her. There was a reason behind it, and it was her only advantage here.

As her vision became sharper, she could make out North was standing over some dead body on the ground, hovering his pistol over it. She didn't know who it was but guessed it was just another unfortunate individual who had somehow crossed paths with him and thus lost his life. Ripley could sense someone pushing her forward as North turned, walking into the building behind him. From what she could gather, it seemed like another abandoned warehouse, given its run-down condition, surrounded by a bunch of old crap people had dumped on it over the years.

Ripley turned to the person dragging her in, trying to gain insight into what was happening. "Hey, what's your name?" she whispered. Except the guy looked away, pretending he never heard, as he heaved her into the warehouse.

The inside of it looked no better, only more decrepit. Parts of the roof had already broken off, as had some of the walls ripped up alongside the floor. The place looked shit. It was a miracle no one hadn't already demolished the site. Still, none of it bothered North, who stood in the centre, smiling. He tucked his pistol away, figuring he would be in the clear for a while, and he was right, of course. Ripley's last viable lead was his loft hideout. It meant chances of a rescue were out of the question unless Harper could track her down, but she doubted it, not with North's skills. He knew how to find places like this, disused, unpopulated, in some back-street site with zero cameras or security that no one wanted to spend any money on protecting.

Ripley was on her own. There was no changing it, so she had to make the most of her opportunity with the man himself.

North turned towards her, pulling up one of the broken chairs from the floor. "Tie her down to it," he barked.

The other man followed suit, forcing her onto the chair before using some of the rope he took from the vehicle to secure her. Ripley stared fixed at the cracked ground as she tried to regain her focus. She kept her mind active, replaying everything she knew about North. She reviewed all the missions he had served on, the bodies he left behind, and the victims he had murdered and wounded long before today. All the facts, details, stories, the rumours she'd ever read or heard about him. As she poured through the information, focusing her attention, she remembered what Steve had mentioned about the second man.

"Is it Matthew?" she asked, adjusting her sights to face him.

Matthew stood in a daze, looking at her, spooked, unsure how she would possess his name. Ripley surmised from his dauntless expression that he was still pretty fresh to all this, compared to North, and lacked his level of conviction. She realized he was the weak link between her two captives, so this sliver of insight gave her an edge she needed to find a way out.

"How do you know my name?" he asked, hiding his anxiety. But, unfortunately, Ripley didn't have time to answer as North, listening in, realised her game and yanked Matthew away, not wanting to give her an advantage.

"Hey, you're not talking with her. Wait outside. In fact, move that stupid surveyor I killed and examine that van of his. We may have a use for it."

Matthew looked back, knowing it was pointless to argue with him, and nodded, accepting his order.

Alone to do what he pleased, North strolled in front of Ripley, towering over her. She tried to straighten herself up, showing him no sign of fear, but North just smirked in delight, seeing the fire in her.

"I take it since you know his name, you'll know mine."

"I know who you are, David North," she said with strength.

North chuckled as he shuffled back, prying out her ID card, flashing it in her face. "That's okay because I know yours, Miss Naomi Ripley. I presume you're not married, given the line of work you're in."

Ripley shrugged the comment off, knowing he was baiting for a line and wouldn't fall for his trap.

"Alright, let's not waste any time here. How did you find me?" North said, void of any humour, placing her ID away. He examined Ripley's expression, waiting for her to respond. Still, she remained serene despite his piercing gaze. Her instincts told her he was seeking something from her, something specific only she must have known about. Otherwise, he would have left her for dead or taken any of the officers if he desired a hostage. Ripley figured she could use this to her advantage in learning about his plan.

"We tracked your movement from where you murdered the second target back to your hideout," she said, wondering if he would believe her lie, but North just burst out in laughter.

"We were both trained by the same people, who spent a lot of time and money teaching us the tricks to avoid detection. So, the only way you could have tracked me like that was if I was sloppy, and I mean extremely sloppy," North said, leaning forward, grasping at her face. "Now tell me, do you think I'm that stupid?"

Ripley stared at his sadistic, mocking face for what felt like an eternity before shaking herself free from his hold.

North just snickered at her tenacity, clasping her chin to force her eyes to meet his. "So, tell me, girl, how did you find me? Really."

Ripley paused, realising she needed to be smarter with her responses. Weak answers like she'd given weren't good enough to fool him. So, using the only piece of relevant info she knew, she came up with another approach for finding out something substantial about his plan.

"How about a trade? Answer for an answer. Tell me how many more MPs you plan to murder; I'll tell you how we found your hideout," she suggested.

North stepped back, pondering her request as he examined her conditions. He saw the spirit in her eyes, but in reality, she was a shattered woman, incapable of standing on her own two feet without support. He figured there was no harm in telling, believing it would help her open up to what he wanted from her.

"Alright, I'll bite. I only have one prick of a politician left to kill, truth be told."

Ripley studied his response, replaying his voice-over, judging each word, the tone he said it in. She tried to determine if there was any truth in the answer or just a bunch of bullshit as she studied it again and again. However, North soon grew impatient with her silence and lowered himself to her level, eager for her response to his generosity.

Ripley knew she had to give him something to keep him talking, to learn anything substantial about what he was up to by saying what he needed to hear. No matter how much she didn't want to say it, she needed to share it with him.

"Your driver told me where to find you," she said in regret, knowing she'd just put Steve in a dire situation if she didn't survive this mess. Still, her captor didn't mind, he just grinned with delight, thinking he'd cracked her.

"I figured he'd talk. That prick didn't seem as capable as you and me, but who is anymore?" North stated. "So then, what else did that traitor tell you?"

Ripley now understood why North wanted her. Steve must have known something about him that threatened his entire operation. It's why he acted in such a reckless manner by using the explosives with himself in the room. Sure, it gave him a massive thrill ride like usual, but he could have easily taken his own life. However, people make rash decisions when they're afraid, and North is still human despite his reputation. So, he can still feel fear like anyone, and whatever Steve possessed scared him shitless. The only problem was that he never told her anything meaningful other than his location and that he owned a brand-new suit. From what she gathered, Steve didn't seem to know anything remarkable about North. There was no way he was lying. By the end of their conversation, he was too afraid of losing his mother to hold anything back.

Ripley figured Steve perhaps wasn't even aware he possessed something this damaging to North that he'd risk abducting someone to find out. Still, it gave her something to play with as she glimpsed into his eyes, seeing the modest twinkle of fear he'd tried to cast away. She sensed North wasn't in complete control. She knew he should've continued hunting for his last target instead of kidnapping her. His behaviour was all out of character, so it should, in theory, lead him to make mistakes, allowing her to stop him if she were to play it right.

"Oh, nothing much. He wasn't that helpful. As you said, it's difficult to find decent help these days," she remarked.

"No doubt about it, I rarely work with others. I much prefer to handle this shit myself. It's simpler that way. However, time was of the essence, and in this case, I needed the support, so you have to work with what's available. It's a shame you weren't free. I would've loved to have someone like you on this job."

"I don't think you can afford me. My rate's pretty high, you know."

"Oh, I believe you're worth it, whatever the price. You strike me as a real go-getter, even if you are on the wrong team, but we're all young and misguided once, so I won't hold it against you.

"Ah, and there's me thinking you had no heart, but, then again, people like you never do."

"Funny. Give it a few years; you'll start seeing this life for what it is. – Trust me. It will change you, but not for the better."

"Maybe, but I doubt you'll live long enough for me to prove you wrong, you know, given how you don't seem to be on top of your game right now," she added with a touch of sarcasm.

North masked his resentment over her comment as he reassessed her, knowing he'd have to be more direct now, less playful, in order to get his information.

"Out of curiosity, how long have you been a government slave?"

"Seven months, asshole."

"Oh, you're lucky. You're still in that lovely sweet spot where you're still duty-bound, filled with that honour and deep patriotic love for your country that only Americans seem to think they have." North said as he closed in on Ripley, losing any sense of the joy he had. "Ahead of that point, when the job starts to break you down on such a personal level, then in an instant, without realising it, any chance of ordinary life disappears forever. That's what awaits you, my friend, your future if you continue to stand with those worthless pieces of scum. They don't care about you – or ever will – no matter how many times you save their ass."

Ripley viewed him with no emotion, not letting him get inside her head as he stared into her with those black unblinking eyes of his. She knew his game, trying to scare her, make her feel hopeless, alone through all his talk, his lies. Brutes like him had been trying the same thing on her all her career, but she never gave in to them, and wasn't starting now. She was better than that.

"Not everyone can, but maybe you couldn't just cope. Ever think about that, you prick?"

North retaliated like a muscle reflex, smacking her right across the jaw for her remark. Still, like countless times before, Ripley held her nerve as her captor clenched her face harsher than ever.

"Me coping had nothing to do with it. On the contrary, I loved the job more than you could ever imagine. It gave me a purpose in life when I needed it most. Still, after years of risking your life and sanity for these so-called bosses, there's nothing left for you." North tightened his grip, digging his nails into her cheeks, forcing her to stare into his gaze, his truth. "No support, respect, or even a proper wage, just some meaningless pat on the back from some suit-wearing prick who still lives with mummy and daddy. I'd had enough of their idiocy and so ventured out to use my talents for myself for once, free from anyone's control, so I could earn the admiration and wealth they had rightfully denied me for all those years of glorified service!"

Ripley stared back at him, seeing through the self-pity charade bullshit he held himself to and wasn't taking any of it. "You're nothing but a murderer, blaming the world for your problems. You choose to only see this life in terms of money, killing, and glory when it's so much more than that! It's about the people: the innocent individuals we pledge to protect from the fanatics, the psychopaths, the murderous pricks of this world who'd harm them, just like you, North, you worthless excuse of a soldier!"

Flustered, North stared back in utter silence, unsure how to respond, having lost his momentum, with her words still flickering around his ears. He couldn't say why they stung so hard, but they did; they just did, no matter how much he resisted admitting it. Then, after a few moments, he let out a slight groan and struck Ripley straight across the face, knocking her so hard she toppled back onto the floor. He then stood up, leaving the room, rubbing his head in frustration over the knots growing in his stomach.

Ripley, meanwhile, laid on the ground cautiously optimistic with herself as blood slowly trickled down her newest split lip, knowing she'd struck his nerve.

Chapter 21

North paced back and forth for minutes. He slapped himself in the face over and over again as he gathered himself, erasing all trace of her words, her accusations from his mind. Then, needing a distraction to calm himself, he concentrated all his efforts on the task at hand, thinking about how best to tackle the situation.

It was apparent Ripley wasn't about to give in just yet. Despite being caught in the explosion, she still had a lot of strength. He admired it a bit, remembering how he used to be in the old days; still, it left him in a precarious position. He'd bought himself a bit of time, just not enough to tear her body apart, to determine what Steve had told her about the last target, if he even knew. It was driving him insane. If Steve had seen Singh's face on the screen, did he understand its significance? Was he clever enough to connect the dots to know whether it was a target or not? The entire job was in complete free fall because this one guy might have seen something on his laptop.

North stomped the ground in frustration as he replayed it all over in his mind again. He tried to remember the direction Steve was facing, his distance from the screen, how long he stood there, and where his eye line was. He kept repeating it, over and over, hoping he'd missed something, anything, but he didn't. Every time he replayed the incident, it kept pointing at Steve having a partial view of the screen.

In theory, in the few seconds, before it closed, Steve could've glanced at Singh's face. Still, even at a cursory glance, would he have recognised who it was? Or, to him, would it just be some random Indian guy on the web? North debated about it hard, brushing his hands across his face, scrutinising it, time and time again, as he rested them on the back of his neck. He finally gave himself the time to examine his blunder without the threat of an imminent attack rushing him.

He gripped his neck for what felt like hours, stomping around in a tiny circle. He disputed each point in his mind, trying to determine the most probable outcome of this mess. In the end, North released his neck, concluding that even if Steve remembered the face, he wouldn't be able to place it. His chance to register it as a target was far too low in just a few seconds. Singh's not some high-ranking MP whose had his face smeared in the media for saying some crap he shouldn't have. He was at most an amateur mid-level player whose only significant achievement in his, surprisingly, long career was to scare his employer into needing him dead.

Singh would still carry on with his typical day like nothing was wrong, providing North with the chance to kill him. The odds weren't in his favour, they never were, yet the job had to be completed, regardless. It wasn't even about the money for his dwindling retirement plans because if he fled today, word would spread fast. His reputation, the respect he'd built for years, would disappear overnight. After that, jobs would forever stop coming his way, thinking him out of practice, no longer the daredevil he once was. It's why he was so unwilling to reach out to his old comrade for support. He didn't want to appear weak, like he'd lost his capability or control of the situation; if he did, his life would be meaningless and he'd have nothing. He'd have no purpose outside of trying to overcome the stigma of being a failure, a coward who could no longer do the one thing he excelled at. No matter what, North promised himself he wouldn't let that happen. He would kill Singh and stay untainted by this looming shame of his indiscretion.

Matthew was busy inspecting the surveyor's van as ordered but was regularly checking over at North pacing around. There was a sense of unease about him as if he was worried about everything panning out as he tried to think of a solution. He then glanced towards the warehouse, knowing the agent inside knew his name. It meant the rest of the security forces also knew. His ordinary life was over. He would have to adapt to North's way of living to survive now. It would mean heading out into the world and using his talents to make a name for himself. It was a daunting task, but Matthew didn't have another choice. He couldn't return to delivering goods from one warehouse to another; there was more to living than that. His time in the military gave him a pure glimpse of it. Life was far more dynamic and fulfilling for those three years of service than anything he'd ever experienced, despite never firing his weapon. He missed it, the action, the adventure, the glory of it all. He knew working for North was his one chance to feel that way again, and it would be worth it, in every sense of the phrase. Fuelled by this notion, he decided to hell with it; he would confront North, regardless of the consequences.

Matthew stood tall, walking over to him.

"What's the plan then?" he asked, standing his ground with authority.

North just gazed back with enthusiasm, impressed that he could finally see Matthew's backbone instead of the panicky state he'd been in all day. "We're not leaving, not until the target is dead. We're finishing the job."

Matthew didn't flinch, suspecting that would be the case, but he was ready for it. Whatever it was, he was ready. "Alright, what's our next move, then?"

North grinned back, figuring Matthew was finally ready to prove his worth to him. He knew it wouldn't take long before the thrill of the job captured him, as it did for him in the desert so long ago.

"That prick's van. Is it all good?"

"It's fine. The guy kept it in pristine condition."

North patted him on the shoulder, sensing the plan he was hatching coming to life. "Well, that worked out well for us, not so much for him. Wrong place, wrong time, as they like to say."

Matthew nodded back in agreement. "Yeah, he picked the worst day to stop by this place. So, what is your plan?"

"Simple, we create another distraction," North said, waving Matthew to follow him back inside the warehouse. "Let me show you how."

The pair entered, seeing Ripley slumped on the floor, unable to do anything but lay there. On approaching, North signalled for Matthew to lift her. He followed suit, picking her up while she remained strapped to the chair. Once level-headed, North bent down, wiping all the blood off her face with his sleeve. He gazed into her deep green eyes, trying to make her comfortable, like she was his friend.

"Your boss, what's his name?" he said with the sincerest voice he could produce.

Ripley stared at him, masking her confusion at his question, wondering what he was planning. She ran it through her mind, thinking about the angle he might have taken, the schemes he might have devised, what he might try to achieve. Still, nothing obvious came to mind that might pose a danger if she revealed it. Ripley couldn't see his game but realised that whatever he was plotting, she needed to play along to have a chance of stopping.

"Elliot Denver," she pronounced.

North stepped away, smiling as he pulled out an old flip phone. "I take it the old emergency service number is still the same."

Ripley didn't answer, but North could deduce from her stubborn reaction that he was correct. With that, he entered the numbers and waited while it dialled out. After the first ring, the call got picked up and placed straight through to the service operator. North, however, didn't give them a chance to speak.

"Yes, hello there. I was hoping you could connect me with one Elliot Denver, at once. Inform him it's David North, the man responsible for murdering all the MPs today and who is also holding his agent, Naomi Ripley, at gunpoint."

Within seconds, the operator put him through without delay. North grinned with glee as he faced Ripley upon hearing Denver answer him.

"Mr Denver, don't say a word. I know you'll have someone locking on my position, so I'll be quick. I want to do a swap. My driver, you're holding prisoner for your prat of an agent. We'll be in Leicester Square within eighty-five minutes. You bullshit me or don't show, your agent dies screaming, as does every civilian within a ten-foot radius of that area. Does that make sense?"

There was a brief pause as Denver assessed the situation before agreeing to his demands, knowing he didn't have a choice.

"Good, I'll call again in seventy-five minutes with more details for the swap."

North ended the call, splitting the mobile in two and smashing it on the ground for good measure.

Ripley stared at North, whose face was glowing like he had the winning lottery ticket.

"You're actually planning to use the same trick again," she remarked.

North gazed down, smiling at her, sensing he was finally back in control. For the first time since the incident in the loft, he felt like himself again, and no words, no accusations about what he was or is from her could change that. "It's a tried and tested tactic that never fails to work for me, my dear, only requiring a slight tweak for whatever the situation is, so I think I'll be fine."

North turned to Matthew, who straightened up as he looked at him, eager for action. "We're moving. Get her off that chair."

Matthew bent down, untying the ropes before the pair started dragging her out. Ripley avoided causing any resistance. She regained some of her strength back but knew, given her current condition, she wasn't a match against two people, not yet. So, she allowed them to drag her out without a fuss, knowing that the actual fight lay ahead and she'd need everything for it. Once they reached the van, Matthew swung the doors open before North twisted Ripley around, punching her deep in the gut for a lasting memory of their shared time. The wind burst out of her as she stumbled to her knees but made sure not to give North the satisfaction of thinking he'd won. He then threw her into the van, slamming the doors behind her.

The pair smiled, walking over to the three series, where North opened the back seat, passing his gear over to Matthew.

"Here, take the explosives, head to someplace, like Oxford Circus. Find a remote area and plant the explosives with that bitch, then blow it in seventy minutes," North said without the slightest sympathy for any of the innocent bystanders he was about to disfigure. Still, none of it crossed Matthew's mind, only seeing the genius in his plan to fool the security services by having them rushing around London in complete chaos. "Once done, head to Kensington, and I'll call your burner to meet you."

Matthew didn't hesitate to accept the bag from him. "What about the last target? What are we to do about that?"

"Relax, I have a plan to end that bastard's life."

Matthew stared back into his eyes and saw no fear in them. He wasn't backing down, and neither was he. After everything he'd experienced in the last few hours, he had no doubts. This was his moment, his chance to prove his worth, so he was ready to do what was necessary. It didn't matter if it meant murdering innocents in the name of his new life; he was ready.

"Don't worry; you can count on me."

North nodded, shaking him by the hand as an equal, before the pair jumped into their respective vehicles, driving off to finish the job.

Chapter 22

Denver was deep in thought, walking up the stairs into the Section. He had a ticking time clock in front of him now. Another MP would be dead within less than eighty-one minutes, along with Ripley and God knows how many civilians. In particular, if North was to use anything akin to the bomb they recovered from the market or like the ones that took out the CTSF officers, it was all up in the air for him. There were too many moving pieces, all kinds of possibilities with too little certainty anywhere to manage the impending terror. No matter how much he cared for Ripley, the priority had to be stopping North. Otherwise, his carnage would only continue.

Denver knew Ripley would make the same choice in his position. He trusted that somehow, she would do whatever she could on her end to stop North's slaughter from happening herself. It's why he respected her so much. She understood the danger of playing with people's lives in this job. She'd always been able to make the crucial choices few could stop the most severe threats from happening. A trait inherited from her father, where the life of one individual isn't worth the massacre of hundreds, regardless of who that individual is.

Denver entered the Section heading straight for Harper, who, as usual, remained lost in his work and failed to notice when someone approached.

"Alife, tell me you have something," Denver said, hiding his desperation.

Harper looked up at him, grinning. "I have it, Elliot, our smoking gun. Look."

Denver leaned over as Harper adjusted his monitor for him to see the footage of the charity ball. He didn't have to figure it out as Harper pointed right towards the major attraction. The home secretary sat in a secluded corner with the second dead MP, talking and laughing with a handful of other individuals. They'd found them, the like-minded colleagues Mrs Wilson spoke of. However, it meant that any of these laughing people that were all jollying it up in the footage, living life to its fullest, had the potential to be dead in the next seventy-eight minutes. Still, it meant they were no longer blind to North's prey as Harper looked up, seeing Denver smile for the first time today.

"Fortunately, the good news doesn't stop there," he chirped.

Harper flipped through the screens, zooming in while Denver wondered what he was about to see. He bought up more footage from the party, offering from another angle a gentleman on his own standing across the room gazing at the group, visibly infuriated with himself. Denver couldn't help but recognise the face of Malcolm Abbot, aka the axeman within parliament. It's a nickname he earned over twelve years ago after becoming known as the man you call when you have a political problem to sort out; no one else could. He would straighten it out no matter how shitty it was, never caring who he had to piss off. The downside was that it often led to Abbot making a lot of enemies within the opposition and sometimes his own party. Still, his one redeeming quality was forever being a true loyalist to his coalition. The man had served in government for over a third of his adult life. His efforts and influence helped secure the party to power years ago, earning him a fancy private corner office at number ten. However, that wasn't the same person who occupied it now. Abbot was like an old dog no one wanted to put down. People still liked him to a certain degree, but he didn't have the same bark as in the old days.

"That dodge bastard," Denver said in a digest. Harper looked at the man and shared his displeasure.

"I've cross-referenced his records, and there is a connection to North. They both served in the same regiment back in their old army days, with Abbot being one of his superiors. From what footage I've gathered, he seems to argue with several members of the group during the night. So, I'm guessing this entire mess must have spawned from there."

Denver patted Harper on the back. He'd found the man behind the assassin, and knowing it could be the key needed to stop the massacre from coming.

"Exceptional work here, Alife. We have to assume all these people are in danger. Contact number ten to have them placed under security ASAP and inform them I'm heading down. It's time I talked with the axeman."

Chapter 23

North had made his last change of clothes of the day, finally removing his workman overalls into what was a decent suit. It was nothing high-end or fancy, just whatever Steve had bought him in the morning. It made him look more professional like he was a functioning member of society, and that was the point. He wore it with stride, strolling down the street as if he was a different person. He passed the houses by, realising it was the type of street no average working-class member could afford, not on the current hourly wage. Still, for a member of Her Majesty's government, they could splash out for a home in Kensington from all the unofficial salaries and pay-outs they collected behind closed doors.

North had determined from his employer's itinerary that Singh would be in parliament all day thanks to back-to-back meetings. Since none of them was outside, trying to kill him that way was out of the question, given his current time frame before the city descended into chaos. In particular, with all the attention on him, trying to sneak into parliament was just a no-go option, even for someone with his talents. Moreover, he knew their security would have tightened up by now. With all the extra eyes, he wouldn't be able to get close to the target, let alone smuggle his Glock in. Fortunately, North had devised the ideal plan to draw him out into the open. All it would take was applying the correct amount of external pressure on the situation.

North approached the front of the last house on the edge of the street, stopping to scan his surroundings. He was alone; there were no dog walkers, delivery drivers or even a jogger nearby. There was nothing but silence, the perfect setting for him to execute his scheme. North smiled, straightening his tie-up once more before he walked up the steps, knocking on the front door. Nineteen seconds passed before a young woman opened the door, wearing an apron covered in flour stains from all her baking. She graciously greeted him with her sweet maternal smile.

"Hi, how may I help?" she said.

North smiled back, making himself appear as friendly as possible to fool her. "Hello Mrs Singh, my name is Freddie. I work on behalf of Her Majesty's security services," he said, flashing the ID card he took from Ripley to help prove his authenticity which, to his credit, she believed. "There has been a situation with your husband, and they've sent me to keep an eye on you."

The woman's smile vanished in the blink of an eye. Her mind became flooded with all these disturbing thoughts about what might have happened to her husband.

"Oh my god, what's happened to him?"

North tried to ease her by saying, "it will be much easier if I discuss this with you inside."

She wiped away the tears forming in her eyes, remembering her manners. "Yes, of course," she said, gesturing him into the house.

For his own sake of mind, though, to keep his knots at bay, North took one last glance behind him, and to his delight, it was still silent. No one was around. As far as he could tell, not a single person in the capital knew he was here, and he couldn't help but snicker about it.

North closed the door as soon as he stepped inside. He followed Mrs Singh through the hallway into the kitchen, dropping any notion of hilarity, remaining the professional he appeared to be. As soon as he walked in, he spotted a toddler sitting in the corner doing some doodles in a Paddington Bear colouring book. The child was blissfully unaware of his presence as North stood beside him, watching him add some colour to his strange-looking drawings of the bear from Peru. The fact that he wasn't staying in the lines didn't bother him; he seemed to enjoy getting lost in his little world.

"How old is the child?" he asked.

The woman wiped her face again as she looked at her son, wondering if he still had a father or not.

"He's two."

"Ah, what an age to be. Still too young to know what this world is like beyond what we tell them. Do you have any other children?"

"Only the one. We plan on having a second one — but please, can you tell me what's happened to my husband?"

North remained calm as he approached, looking around the kitchen for signs of any other occupant. "Of course, Mrs Singh, but first, can you inform me if anyone else in the household might need to be made aware of this?"

A faint smile broke across her face. "You can call me Latakia, and no, it's just the two of us."

North kept a straight face as he lunged over, grabbing Latakia by the neck and rushing her back against the wall. After that, he drew his Glock, drilling it into the front of her cheeks. Her entire body turned white, scared out of her wits, oblivious to what was happening.

"You make any noise or attempt to run away; your child will watch his mother bleed out to death. Is that clear?" North stated.

It only took her a millisecond, but Latakia nodded back in agreement at his grotesque request.

"Good, very good. All I need from you is one simple favour. Call your husband and let me speak to him."

Latakia looked back, confused over what he needed her to do, but nodded in agreement, knowing she would do anything if it meant protecting her son's existence.

North released her, stepping back as she plummeted to the ground.

Latakia slowly got to her feet as North aimed his pistol at her, grabbing her mobile off the charging station and dialled her husband. After a few rings, it went straight to voicemail, and at that moment, the look of horror grew on her face. All these horrendous images of her death or, more disturbingly, seeing this stranger do something to her son swamped her mind in rapid succession. She hit the redial button, pushing the images aside, praying to her gods that he'd pick up.

North stood, staring at her with a steady gaze, his grip slowly tightening around the handle, while his index finger lingered over the trigger, waiting to press it. He knew if this didn't work out, he'd have to move on to his alternative of scouting out parliament and killing Singh once he finished for the day. After he had dealt with his wife and child to ensure they wouldn't warn him, of course. Still, North took his time. He knew deep down that this strategy would work for him and save him from this looming shame he felt. So, he let Latakia call the number again and again.

The dial tone buzzed out for what felt like aeons ahead of Singh, finally picking up after three more attempts. Latakia burst into tears upon hearing his voice, powerless to control herself.

"Anil, there's a man here . . ."

But, she couldn't finish her plea once North moved in. First, he smacked her across the face with his pistol, causing her to crash onto the floor. Then he snatched hold of the mobile as Latakia scrounged over to her son, clenching him tight as her forehead dripped with blood.

"Mr Singh, be quiet and act natural. Don't speak until you're in a place where no one will overhear you, and, for your family's sake, do it right now," North demanded.

A strange stillness descended in the kitchen over the next few seconds as North listened to Singh's pitiful excuses, waiting for him to step aside from his supposed meeting.

"Alright, I'm alone. Now, where is my wife?" he cried, restraining his anger, trying to remain level-headed in the face of this disturbing situation.

North turned towards Latakia, who'd curled up in a corner with her son and smiled at them.

"Both your wife and child are alive, for now, but only if you do as I want, and what I want is for you to leave parliament and come straight home, alone. I don't care what excuses you give, do it now. Otherwise, your family dies screaming."

North raised his pistol and fired a blind shot into the corner where Singh's family cowered. Not close enough to hurt either of them, but close enough so they got the full blast of a suppressed bullet vibrating into their eardrums. North held the mobile towards them, letting Singh hear their screeches of terror. He wondered if this little stunt would motivate him to do what he needed without question, or if he'd need to try something more harrowing instead.

"Is that clear?" North asked once their screams had subsided.

There was a brief pause as the line grew silent. Singh's heart sank as the echoes of his family's squeals flickered across his mind over what this stranger had done to those dearest to him. He wanted nothing more but to call out to them, to make sure they were okay, unharmed, but he knew that wasn't possible, not with a man like this. Singh heard that unsettling calmness in his voice as he made them shriek in terror. There was no way to negotiate with what he desired, and he knew it. Still, regardless of whatever this stranger craved from him, he wasn't about to do anything to jeopardise his family's lives. His family was everything to him, particularly his son, an innocent child who didn't deserve to have his entire future murdered by some random stranger.

"Yes, it is," he responded after gathering his composure.

North lit up upon hearing his submission. He had applied the correct amount of pressure, and his strategy to draw out his last target was a roaring success.

"Excellent. Oh, and remember, I'm watching the streets, so any notion of foul play, your family dies, and it won't be quick. I'll make sure they suffer, and suffer, starting with your little boy here, before I move on to his blessed mother. You got that."

Another slight pause from Singh followed as the total weight of the atrocious situation drowned him further into despair. At some point, he tried to speak, fighting through the bulging lump forming in his throat for his family's sake. "I . . . I understand," he replied with what semblance of resolve remained.

"Well then, get moving, and don't hang up. I want to make sure I hear everything."

North, filled with delight, placed the mobile on the counter, switching it to the speaker as he pulled a stool up, sitting down to listen to Singh's movements. His gaze fixed on the corner of the room where his wife clasped her child for dear life. Her heart ached at the thought of what horrors awaited them and her husband as she prayed that her son would survive the outcome, no matter what it meant for her.

Chapter 24

Under Denver's command, security forces stormed Abbot's office hard and fast. He never saw it coming as they ploughed through the door. He was sitting at his desk alone, waiting for the message that North had done it, but it didn't matter. Once he heard the hinges snap off the door, he knew it was over. Still, it didn't stop him from attempting a last-ditch escape, trying to climb out of his window, but he was just too slow. Years ago, he was in peak physical condition. The routine from his earlier career in the military helped him maintain his stature, spending over an hour every day working out. However, he wasn't the same man anymore. The increasing pressures of a life spent behind a desk and the recent shortcomings in his career left no time or energy to exercise. After a while, he'd lost all motivation to work out, so eventually, it stopped altogether. Then, as time rolled by, his speed, along with his muscles, slowly faded away. He could only muster the smallest amount of resistance as the security forces clawed him back into the office.

Denver entered once he was subdued, towering over him as he lay face down on the floor. Then, with a snap of his fingers, he signalled for Abbot to come up. The security forces followed as commanded, forcing him onto one of the guest chairs. Denver stared at him with disgust at everything he'd done. He never had much love for Abbot during his career. He'd always backed budget cuts in the military and security department as revenge for being repeatedly passed over for promotion during his time in service. It's a grudge; he always reminded them of any time they needed help from the government on sensitive matters.

Despite this, Denver still respected the man. He was true to his word, the sort of person who still believed in the sacred trust created by shaking another's hand. He was forever the person you could rely on to fight in your corner, even if it was a losing battle. It often came at a cost, though, usually in someone losing their seat or livelihood, but he'd now crossed a line he'd never be able to revoke.

"It's time for this to end, Abbot. Tell me where North is," Denver demanded.

Abbot just sat there in silence. He couldn't even bring himself to look at Denver. He had lost, but only now did it dawn on him. All the death, the misery he'd caused over the last few hours, was for nothing. In the end, he still lost.

Denver didn't need long to realise how fragile Abbot was. He didn't hide it, struggling to hold his tears at bay, turning into a mess in front of everyone. Still, time was against him, and smacking Abbot around wouldn't get him anywhere. He was too emotionally unstable, capable of clamming up at any moment. Denver knew it would require a different course of action, so he signalled the security forces to leave the room. They positioned themselves outside as Denver walked over, shutting the door and leaving him alone with the axeman. After a sigh, Denver turned back. Abbott sat in his chair with his head in his hands, quietly sobbing, distraught over what he had done.

"We know you were in the same unit as North back in your old army days, Malcolm. You might even think of him as a friend, but it's time for this insanity to end before more innocent lives perish."

Abbot did his utmost to pull himself together as he wiped away his tears, looking up at Denver. "I was desperate. You must understand that, I tried everything and everyone, and this was it. This was my last chance to survive."

Denver pulled up a chair from his desk, sitting beside him in a friendlier manner to help ease his nerves.

Abbot looked at him, sniffling into his jacket, wiping the snot bubbles away. "I've been a member for nearly twenty years. I did all they asked of me; no matter what it took from me professionally or personally — I did it."

Denver shuffled in closer and nuzzled Abbot across his back to ease his discomfort.

"I found out at the charity ball that the secretary and his friends planned to phase me out. They'd found some dirt on me from my younger days and planned to reveal it tomorrow in parliament. It's a death sentence. The PM would have had no choice but to throw me out of the party I helped him build. In short, everything I've dedicated my life to, everything I sacrificed for my coalition, would have ultimately led to nothing." Abbot pulled some tissues out from his pocket as he started weeping more heavily, wiping away the mess foaming around his face.

Denver watched, masking his contempt, allowing Abbot to maintain his composure long enough for him to continue.

"I tried to convince some of them against it. I pleaded with them to stop, but they wouldn't listen. None of them would. I offered them money, continued political support, and endless favours, but nothing. It was as if I were talking to a brick wall. They wouldn't budge, not one bit. Then, I became so desperate that I . . . I turned to North."

Abbot paused, realising it was at this moment from days ago that he destroyed his life. In retrospect, he could have graciously accepted the loss and still walked away into some form of early retirement with the freedom to enjoy his life. Instead, his legacy would only now be a trail of bloodshed and mayhem, all from this single choice.

"North's helped me out in the past, with smaller jobs, and has always come through for me. He told me he could deal with them if I supplied him with details of their itineraries. However, I didn't know he'd do anything this reckless," he said as tears trickled down his cheeks, thinking about those who'd died from his choice. He, then stared at Denver, his eyes turning red, begging him to believe that whatever he may think, he never wanted this carnage or bloodshed. All he wanted was to hold on to the minor success he had achieved in his life.

Denver stared back, not saying a word. His state made him believe that all this carnage was down to North and North alone. However, he didn't forget Abbot played his part in orchestrating all this. He could have stopped if he so desired. Come clean when the news hit about all the innocent people who'd died, taking responsibility for what had happened, still showing some level of human decency.

Abbot had plenty of blood on his hands, and Denver knew he would have to confront his own mistakes on his own. Still, if he was seeking his forgiveness, he wasn't about to receive it. Nonetheless, he kept comforting him, suppressing his disdain, for he had a job to do, lives to save.

"It's okay, Malcolm. It's okay. You can stop this from escalating any further. Just tell me where to find North," he asked.

Abbot put himself together as best he could before he turned to look at Denver, sorrow all over his face. "I don't know how to find him. I never have. We've only ever spoken via an email system he'd set up years ago," he said.

Denver ceased patting. He lowered his arm to his side, hiding his disappointment as he looked away, trying to think about how to recover from the situation. He glanced at his watch, seeing that he had thirty-eight minutes left before North's deadline, and bodies would start piling up.

They both sat in a dull silence, where the only noise produced came from Abbot, sobbing into his sleeve. He had ruined his tissues, knowing there was no way out for him. Denver pondered over everything in his mind, trying to determine his next step and all the other avenues available to him. He considered all the people he could turn to, all the favours he could request, or schemes he could use to find North that was still open to him. He needed something, anything, that could help prevent the carnage from approaching. In repeating the vast amount of information to himself countless times over, Denver realised there was something Abbot said that didn't align with his train of thought.

"You said you tried to convince some of them to stop." Abbot raised his head, gazing at him. "We're all the secretary's friends' targets?" he asked.

"No, only the senior people. The others wouldn't have the guts to risk everything if they weren't involved. Not all of them are ambitious."

A small smile broke on Denver's face. He had less than thirty-four minutes to prevent the massacre from happening.

"Who's left?"

"Err, Singh, Anil Singh, he's the last one."

Denver had it, his chance to stop North and maybe save Ripley if she was still alive.

He stood up, leaving the office. Once outside, he ordered the security forces to remove Abbot and confine him inside a cell until further notice. They all nodded without hesitation, stepping inside and hauling him out while he walked off in the opposite direction, never glimpsing back. Denver knew that no matter how the government planned to spin this, he was adamant about making sure Abbot paid for every one of his crimes. He may not have pulled the trigger, but he was equally responsible for each person's death today as North and would ensure that no back-end politics were hiding this.

Denver walked away, pulled out his mobile and dialled the Section. "Harper, listen, we were looking at this wrong. North is only targeting one last MP, Anil Singh. We must find and get him to a secure location at once."

There, however, was a brief pause before Harper could respond, hating the words he was about to utter. "Elliot, Singh's missing."

Denver stopped in his tracks, realising it may be too late to do anything to prevent North from succeeding.

"What happened?"

"No one knows. I was trying to locate all the targets when security informed me that Singh had walked out of a meeting about sixteen minutes ago, but he never returned. Since then, I've been searching for him via CCTV cameras, but it will still take me a few minutes before I find him."

Denver started walking out of the building, shaking off the loss, trying to regain control over the situation.

"We have no choice but to assume this is North. It may not look like it, but we still..."

Unfortunately, Denver didn't have time to finish after Harper interrupted him as someone attempted to transfer an urgent call over. He braced himself, thinking this might be it. It was the message he'd been dreading since he saw North's face on the computer screen all those hours ago, that he had prevailed once again.

"Elliot, it's Ripley! I'm patching you through to her."

Chapter 25

The single light inside the back of the van beamed on Ripley as she rolled around. Still tied up, she knew what was coming. The van would soon arrive at its destination, and Matthew would carry out whatever orders North had given him. Unfortunately for him, Ripley wasn't about to offer him the chance to do anything. She'd always been a fighter; as long as there was oxygen in her lungs and blood in her veins, she didn't intend to surrender. The first issue Ripley had to overcome was that she couldn't put up much of a fight in her current state. She would need her hands free to stand a chance at taking him on. Ripley scanned the entire interior of the van, but it lacked anything sharp she could utilise to cut through the cables. The only thing that came to mind that she could use was her teeth, but she'd first need her hands out in front of her.

Ripley rolled over, lying on her side before stretching her arms back as far as possible, crouching her legs up into her body. Once they were in the position, she squeezed them through her arms. It was an excruciating process to undergo, considering it was the first time since the blast she'd tried moving her body. Ripley gritted her teeth and held her tongue as hard as possible to avoid screaming her head off and alerting Matthew.

Then, after a couple of minutes of starting and stopping over, internalising her screeches, she finally blocked out the pain, moving her arms out in front. Next came the ties.

Ripley rushed into action, biting down hard, rummaging through the knot with her teeth, trying to loosen it off. Unfortunately, despite her best efforts, the cables were firmly fastened on, making it impossible for her to chew through or even loosen up. However, the situation soon worsened as she felt the vehicle slowing down before completely stopping. Ripley halted biting as she adjusted her gaze to the front of the van on hearing the engine cut off. A couple of seconds passed before the driver's door closing echoed into her eardrum. Matthew was mere seconds away. He was coming. No matter what, Ripley had to fight, free hands or not. Her only advantage was the element of surprise. It was all she had, so Ripley positioned herself closer to the back doors, staring at them, her eyes fixed, waiting.

Four seconds passed before she heard Matthew fiddling with the handle outside. She bent her knees, reading her stance, waiting. Three seconds later, he yanked back the handle, sunlight came streaming in, and Ripley took her chance, rushing forward. She placed her entire weight against the door, treating it as a makeshift battering ram as she slammed it into him.

The force, combined with the sheer surprise, knocked Matthew straight onto the ground as Ripley fell, landing beside him. Her eyes darted around her surrounding, seeing he'd brought her to some random back alley. As expected, the place seemed deserted, with nobody around that could help, but it made no difference. Ripley doubted they would've rushed in to help the damsel in distress even if someone was there. Instead, they would have taken one look at the pair of them and just walked away, not wanting to get involved like any ordinary bystander.

She turned to spot Matthew, who was starting to regain his footing. Ripley had to act fast if she were to survive, so she put every thought about her body's pain away and, fuelled with adrenaline, leapt to her feet. She dashed towards Matthew, shoulder first, slamming straight into him. The move caused him to groan out in pain as his spine banged against the solid brick wall behind him. Keen to keep the pressure up and deny him the chance to counter, Ripley jerked her head back, striking it into his face. In a flash, he became disoriented, giving her a few more precious seconds to attack. She drove her knee straight into his stomach with them, then immediately struck her elbow across his jaw. Ripley was on a rampage and wasn't ready to stop as Matthew stumbled down from all the blows.

Once he hit the ground, she kicked him in the middle of his stomach. Thanks to the boots she was wearing, they added an extra sting before rolling him over, shoving her knee down onto his spinal cord, trying to subdue him. Then, simply by chance, Ripley spotted his pistol sticking out of the back of his jeans. It seemed in all the confusion, he hadn't had the chance to reach for it. Ripley yanked it out, stepping back as she aimed the pistol at him.

"Stay down!" she barked, flipping the safety off.

Matthew tossed over onto his side, gazing up at her beaten, somewhat disoriented, with a suspected broken nose, but without a doctor he wouldn't know for sure. He spat some blood out of his mouth before lying still, humiliated that an unarmed prisoner had beaten him to a pulp, let alone a woman of all people. He'd failed North. There was no hiding it. His brand-new life was over in the blink of an eye as he reluctantly waved back, obeying her command.

Ripley kept the pistol fixed on him as she stepped back, sliding down the adjacent wall. She allowed herself a second to recover and catch her breath as the adrenaline wore off. Ripley glanced around at the ground, scanning for something sharp to use against the cables. She knew it'd only waste time she didn't have if she continued fiddling about with her teeth. Fortunately, she found a few bits of broken glass near her from a discarded bottle. It most likely came from some drunk kids from a recent night out, smashing it on the ground for fun instead of throwing it in the bin, like any responsible person. Still, regardless of the reason, Ripley was thankful that it had happened. She grabbed the thickest piece and started cutting the cables, still clutching the pistol encase Matthew attempted something. Then, after minutes of rubbing it against her wrist, slicing at the cable while carefully trying not to slash herself, Ripley managed to break it apart.

She stood tall, still trying to put aside whatever pain her body was in, as she hobbled over to Matthew, pistol in hand.

"North, where's he heading?" she growled, hovering the pistol over his face.

Matthew looked up, thinking he wouldn't fail for a second time and lose more of his dwindling pride, having regained some sense of the situation.

"I don't know, bitch."

Ripley bent down, grabbing him by his collar while pressing the pistol against his forehead. "Think. Otherwise, I shoot prick."

Matthew stared back with defiance, knowing she didn't intend to do anything, that it was just an empty threat. He knew she'd be subject to the same restrictions he had to adhere to during his tours in Syria regarding prisoners. It meant treating them with the same respect and dignity you would show any armed forces member, no matter what cause or point of view they held. After all, we're all soldiers striving to safeguard our home and way of life from those who wish to destroy it.

As a result, the mere suggestion of any malicious behaviour would cause immediate dismissal or severe repercussions for those involved. This would only become worse if a prisoner turned out to be a victim of abuse. It meant he was free from any harm, and all Ripley could do was spew empty threats. There was nothing she could do.

"Bitch, I don't know. So, why don't you piss off?" he suggested.

Ripley threw him back, displeased, and just stared at him before recognising there was no point playing around. She had to stop North before he reached his last target. Otherwise, his rampage would never end. Ripley aimed the pistol above his left kneecap, firing into it. The bullet ripped through his flesh, cracking the ground on the other side as Matthew bellowed out in agony. She kept him pinned to the ground, pistol pressed against his head, leaning in with her knee on his wound. The pain of it caused him to scream out in sheer misery. After a long few seconds, she felt Matthew realised this wasn't a game, so she raised her knee and smacked him across the face to stop his wailing.

Matthew laid still, blood seeping out, looking at Ripley in complete fear over what might come next. The only thought that raced through his mind was that she would keep doing this. The lack of remorse on her face proved it.

"North's location, or I'll put one in the other leg, and you'll be lucky if you can walk again without crutches," Ripley said without a shred of shame, drilling the pistol further into his forehead.

Matthew stared into those unblinking green pupils, knowing that every word she said rang true. She intended to keep firing bullets at him until he told her or bled out. He had no intention of dying like this, not in some back alley, alone, in a growing puddle of his blood. In spite of everything he had been through today, everything he'd witnessed and felt from North now meant nothing. Instead, all he felt was a single burning desire to continue living this life, no matter how crappy it might be. All he wanted was to live, just live.

"Kensington, somewhere in Kensington, that's all I know. I swear, please," Matthew said, wailing in sheer agony.

Ripley looked at the tears streaming down his face, the pure fear in them, and realised it was probably genuine, given his current predicament. She knew North's style; he wasn't laying out his grand master plan to anyone but himself. Her only hope now lay in the Section, having discovered something that might narrow the search.

"Your mobile. Where is it?" she barked.

Matthew didn't hesitate at the order, tapping the front of his jeans pocket before Ripley shoved her hands inside to retrieve the mobile and the keys to the van. Ripley placed them in her pocket as she stepped off, but not before grasping his palm and pressing it against his bleeding wound.

"Press down hard, and stay awake."

Ripley stood up, dialling through to the service switchboard. After a quick moment, the operator picked up but didn't give her a chance to speak as she shouted down the line.

"Access code Overlook 217. Put me through to the Section, now!"

A handful of seconds passed by before the connection happened.

"Alife, it's Naomi. Zero in on my location, and patch me through to the chief."

"Already patching you through, my dear," he said with delight after hearing her voice as he linked the call in with Denver.

"Ripley, what's your status?" he asked.

"Still standing, chief. Listen, North has one target left. He's heading to Kensington. I don't know where, but tell me you have something that can narrow it down."

At that moment, Ripley stood waiting, hoping they had something, anything really, that could help salvage this situation.

"We have one better. The target's name is MP Anil Singh. Harper check his records and sees what comes up concerning Kensington with him."

Once more, everything fell silent as she waited, listening to Harper tapping his fingers on the keyboard, hunting for the missing piece. Each second that passed only made Ripley more and more anxious. She stood motionless, waiting for him to say something, her ears focused on nothing but the sound of him typing.

"It's his home address. He lives in Kensington," he said.

When she heard Harper's news, her face lit up. North's location was theirs.

"I have a fix on your position, Ripley. You're close, less than a fourteen-minute drive."

Ripley had it, her chance, albeit a slim one, but a chance, either way, to capture North and end this carnage. She turned back, examining Matthew's state, seeing the blood trickling down his leg. She bent down, tucking the pistol away, before unfastening the belt of his jeans. She then wrapped it above the wound, fastening it down as far as possible to cut the blood flow. Ripley didn't want him to die like this. No one, not even her enemies, deserved to die in pure agonising anguish by themselves.

"Help is on the way, I promise," she said before turning around and rushing into the van.

Matthew didn't know what to expect, but he held his wound tight, hoping she wasn't lying.

As Ripley leapt into the driver's seat, she shoved the blade into the ignition, twisting it around.

"Harper, send the route to this mobile and get an ambulance to this location as soon as possible. They'll find North's man, Matthew, bleeding out from a gunshot wound in his left leg above the kneecap."

Harper paused in thought, picturing how the scenario might have happened for the reports.

"I'm on it. You should have the address now," he said.

Ripley started speeding off through the streets as she looked down at the mobile, seeing the route flash up. "I have it."

"Good, I'm contacting CTSFO to have a unit meet you at the house. However, based on their average response time and the distance they'll need to cover, they won't get there before you."

Still, it didn't faze Ripley, who shifted to the higher gear and accelerated through the traffic, towards Kensington, towards North.

Chapter 26

Mr Singh's house was the quietest it had ever been in two years since they'd welcomed a child into it. Even if a plate were to fall, smashing against the ground, the sound created would echo throughout the entire house. Still, apart from Latakia sobbing in the corner, the only meaningful noise you could hear came from her mobile on speaker. Singh had somehow done it. He had made it out of parliament without being stopped and was in a cab home. A short time from now, he would reunite with his family for their final few seconds on this earth.

North sat watching them, waiting for his arrival, listening to the sounds of the road filtering out of the mobile. There was nothing but car horns honking every few seconds, engines roaring at high speed, to the occasional insult the cab driver threw about. In most cases, it was to the driver in front of them for driving too slowly or doing something stupid that nearly caused an accident. It made the kitchen feel like it had a new lease on life, as if it were alive once more.

In spite of all this, his wife kept weeping every so often. She could make out the slightest murmur of her husband sobbing to himself in the back seat. The fear of what might happen to his family plagued his mind. He wanted nothing more but to

189

hold them tight, feel their loving warmth, and know they were okay. It was a sentiment shared by his wife, who cradled their child in her arms, trying to divert his attention away from their captive's sadistic gaze. As for his son, he just gripped his mother with all his strength, unable to understand why she cried so hard and what this stranger with the gun wanted. As he wished, his father was here to comfort her, for he always knew how to make her smile.

North patiently waited in silence, his custom Glock seventeen resting next to him. He kept his finger on the trigger, ready to fire at a moment's notice. He knew it wouldn't be much longer now. Any moment, Anil Singh would step through the front door, and North would again achieve the impossible in killing his last target.

Chapter 27

Ripley dashed through red lights, crossed roads at high speed and even drove across pavements to reach the house. Still, despite a number of near-fatal crashes, she made it to Singh's address within ten minutes without wrecking the van too much. There was no telling if North was keeping watch on the street, but Ripley wasn't taking any chances, keen to avoid drawing his attention, parking a few houses back. She'd found more of his explosives in the front seat but didn't know if that was all of them. Regardless, though, she was keen to avoid walking into another of his trap after having just survived the previous one.

Ripley took a stroll towards the rear of the house to avoid attracting too much attention. Denver had broken down everything they had come across on her drive down. On how North planned to entice Singh out of parliament, to murder him far from the security forces while using her as another distraction. However, this scheme of his had failed and gave her the chance to stop him at last. It wasn't just for herself, but for every individual who died in pursuit of stopping his madness throughout the years.

Ripley reached the side of Singh's house, but there was no sound as she glanced at the front. She figured North would most likely be watching the front door, waiting for Singh to step through so he could gun him down on sight. It made it a non-viable option. The safer route she assessed would be to enter through the back of the house via the garden since it would be less likely to be watched. Ripley circled to the back wall of the garden and, after assessing there were no eyes on her, rushed up against it. She made the slightest amount of noise possible as she climbed up to prevent anyone in the house from noticing. Ripley peeked up over the top, spotting North sitting in the kitchen. She took it as a clear indication that Singh was still alive, knowing that it wasn't his nature to hang around after committing his murders.

It was her moment. North hadn't noticed her, so she took off with care, lifting herself over the wall, and sliding down into the bushes. Thankfully, the garden was full of shrubs of all different breeds. It shielded Ripley as she lay still, listening for the slightest inkling that North may have spotted her, but there was nothing. It was complete silence like she'd never existed. Ripley took it as her cue that North had noticed anything, so she slowly lifted herself, drawing out the Glock she took from Matthew. She crept out of the shrubbery, acting carefully to avoid making any sudden noise or movement as she locked eyes with her target. However, all her stealthy manoeuvres abruptly ended when she heard faint shouting in the distance.

There was no telling where it was coming from, but all Ripley could see, tilting her head, was North twisting around, raising his Glock. It was happening. Singh was home. Ripley guessed he must have just shown up shouting for his family's safety, like any loving parent. It meant he was about to die as

North centred his aim, poised for the kill. Despite this, Ripley didn't hesitate to intervene, not even for a fraction of a second. After everything she'd witnessed today, she wasn't about to let anyone else die in her midst, not again.

She fixed her sights on North's current position and fired two shots. The first bullet smashed through the window, cutting right into North's upper shoulder. As for the second bullet, it just scratched his arm once his reflexes kicked in, allowing him to edge out of the way, plummeting to the ground.

The family screamed in terror as Ripley burst through the broken window, chasing after him. Still, despite her speed, North had already circled out by the time she entered the kitchen, firing off blind shots in all directions. He was panicking, attempting to cover himself with no notion of control, as he scampered down the hallway.

Latakia shielded her screeching child in the corner, trying to protect him as best she could against all the bullets flying around. As she prayed, they would strike her instead of her son.

"Stay down and don't move," Ripley barked as she came past, ducking down to avoid being hit by any ricochets. But unfortunately, she didn't have the time to check on them. North was the priority, so she had no choice but to hope they would be alright, not injured in any lasting way, as she chased after their captor instead.

A deep silence sank into the hallway once the bullets ceased. Ripley crept down it, following the trail of North's bleeding wound.

"North, it's over. No one else needs to die now. Just surrender." she barked.

But, there was no reply, only silence as she edged forward.

"The street's being locked down. There's no escape for you."

Ripley gripped her pistol tighter as she tried to locate him, but it didn't take long before North burst out of the living room. She was about to fire but froze as he did once they came face to face. After that, they both stood there, staring at each other without uttering a single syllable.

The expression on North's face said it all. He was a goner. This was a completely different type of person than the one she met over an hour ago. The man standing in front of her was not in the right frame of mind. He was dripping with mixtures of sweat and blood all over, with nothing but pure, unchecked panic splattered across his face. This was no longer the acclaimed assassin so many feared and respected but some pretender. Ripley's only conclusion was that her wound must have done more damage than she expected, or perhaps, like she'd detected in that building this afternoon, he'd indeed cracked. He lost his self-control and could no longer hold himself together like the countless others who came before.

North stared back at Ripley in utter confusion, not understanding how she could stand there in front of him. His plan, the one he thought was so brilliant and masterful, capable of saving him from all the trouble, the shame he faced, had failed. It had failed. After taking so many precautions, he couldn't comprehend how she still defied the odds and found him. Still, it didn't matter. It was just yet another thing he'd failed to control, behind everything else, he had lost. There was no refuting it as more streaks of blood drizzled onto his shoe below. His arm still stinging in sheer agony from the bullet trapped within, worsening with each passing second of silence as he stared at Ripley at an utter loss.

Then, like a flip of a coin, it changed. It all changed.

In a fit of rage, North raised his pistol, firing blindly in her direction without a clear sense of a target to hit. Following that, he bolted to the door behind him. His survival instincts had kicked in and took control of his body. They overwhelmed him and left him with no sense of direction but to run. It's all North wanted now, to escape. He didn't care if he was leaving Ripley alive. The desire to survive, that pure primitive instinct we all possess, to live beyond the hardships we encounter in those critical moments of life, consumed North as he grabbed the handle.

Ripley darted his shots, dropping to the ground, as she witnessed North swinging the door back, letting the sun's radiant glow fill the room. He moved forward into the light, towards his freedom, but Ripley refused to let him have it. She steadied her mind, aimed her pistol, and fired two more shots.

Each of the bullets ripped through the air within milliseconds before they connected with North's flesh, cutting through his upper right leg. The force of the blows, combined with the immediate agony he felt, propelled North out of the door, stumbling down the stairs to hit the pavement. Ripley stood up, pacing forward, ready to finish the bastard off, ending his rampage once and for all, but she didn't. Ripley stopped dead in her tracks once she reached the living room. Her eyes widened as she stared in horror at Anil Singh lying on the floor. At that moment, as blood dribbled out of his mouth, capturing North didn't seem to matter to her. She knew, given his current injuries, he wouldn't get far. After all, she had just pierced his leg with two of her bullets. Instead, all she cared about was not losing yet another life today.

Ripley rushed over, stowing her pistol as she checked on Singh, trying to find a pulse. Then, by some miracle, perhaps because North wasn't thinking straight, he'd only shot him once in the stomach. He failed to do his trademark close-quarter headshot before the impulse to escape took hold of him. It meant that despite all the blood pouring out, Singh was still breathing, giving her a chance to save him. Ripley yanked some blankets off the sofa next to her, applying pressure to his wound. She kept the blood back with whatever force she could, but it eventually started seeping out. Ripley yanked off more blankets as fast as she could in response, bundling them around the wound as she pressed down with even more force to keep him stable. She held it steady with one hand while she jerked her mobile out to call the Section.

"Harper, I need an ambulance here now. Singh is critical and losing a lot of blood."

There was a brief pause as he typed away on his keyboard. "They're on route, ETA about nine minutes."

"Are you serious? Is there nothing closer?" she asked.

"I'm afraid not. That's the closest to you, but CTSFO is still on route to help before that."

Ripley didn't have the chance to reply, dropping the mobile as blood trickled through her grip. She instead placed her other hand back on the wound to help reinforce the pressure, holding it steady as she waited.

Singh was losing consciousness, yet he still tried to stand, yearning towards the door, but Ripley nuzzled him down. She knew from her own experience that any unwanted movement he did now was liable to cause more harm and rupture any of his wounded organs. He was also likely to lose any more blood that wasn't already spewing out.

She took her time to lower him back onto the floor, but as she did, he wept in a low voice, "My family, are they safe?"

Ripley thought back, realising she had no clue. She glanced at them when she was in the kitchen a couple of minutes ago, but anything could have happened by now. Any of North's bullets could have easily ricocheted off the walls, striking them. For all she knew, they were bleeding out just like him at this precise moment, and there was nothing she could do about it. She considered calling out to check on them but decided against it. She didn't want to worry him if it was bad news or, worse yet, let his family see him like this since it wouldn't be healthy for anyone.

Ripley instead leaned into him, saying, "Yes, they're fine, but you need to conserve your strength."

She kept him still, giving him something to hold out for, as she squeezed down on the blankets with all her strength, waiting for support to arrive. It was all she could do, and she knew it.

Chapter 28

Some of the longest minutes of Ripley's life passed by her as she struggled to contain his bleeding. She could feel Singh's pulse reducing in beats with every click of his watch. He was on the verge of slipping away, but Ripley didn't surrender. She instead kept her hands pressed against his wound, holding firm despite the blood oozing out. She reflected on the child from the kitchen, knowing from her past ordeals that he'd want both parents in his life if he were still alive. She'd spent half her life without either one, never knowing the mother who'd died in labour bringing her into this world.

From that point, it was just her and her father, in between his countless missions. Still, despite his dedication to the people under his command, he always kept Ripley close by, never wanting to leave her alone. Due to this, their time together was some of the happiest of Ripley's life. It wasn't because of all the different vibrant countries she visited, but because whenever he wasn't on his missions, he was by her side as her father, not a soldier. He taught her about life, valuing the world, the people within it, the virtues every day offers, to every joyous moment in between. No matter how exhausted or battered he was, he made time for her and no one else. It was something Ripley never appreciated until after his death. After that, it was just her, alone, with no other family. All she had was a rotating door of her father's comrades caring for her until she was old enough to sign up herself. Still, for the success she achieved in life, she would trade it all for a chance to see either parent again. It didn't matter if it was for a mere second to hold her father one more time, to hug him tight and say goodbye, or finally, to say hello to her mother for the first time. It's a never-ending ordeal she wouldn't wish on any other child, especially the one so full of life in the framed pictures around her. However, as the minutes dragged on, her salvation came as she heard the screams of sirens filling the street outside. Moments later, CTSF officers poured into the house. Support had finally arrived and may have the tools needed to give that child his father.

"I need a medic kit in here now," Ripley barked out at the officers behind as they entered. Whatever they could do to halt the bleeding until paramedics arrived was vital to keeping Singh alive.

Ripley couldn't hear their response amidst all the noise around her. She could only hear one of them screaming for two people whose call signs she couldn't make out to come into the room. Two officers entered the living room within thirteen seconds following the call. They holstered their weapons and crouched beside Ripley, looking over Singh's worsening condition. Then, without a moment's thought, one of them reached out and rested her palm on Ripley's shoulder. As Ripley turned, she looked into her clear blue eyes to see the officer remove the neck gaiter, masking her face. She then brushed the blonde strands hanging out of her helmet from her face so Ripley could see the officer in full.

"Hey, listen, my name's Jodie. We're trained medics. You've done brilliant work here, in every sense of the term, outstanding work. However, it will be better for him if we take over. It's time. You've done everything you can to help," she said as calmly as her voice would allow, ensuring Ripley would understand every point of what she was asking her for.

Ripley gazed down at Singh, sensing his pulse dipping out of rhythm with each beat of her own heart. As he grew more still, less responsive, she realised that she had done everything to keep him alive, but she couldn't save him, not like this. Despite her efforts, the blood seeping out of him was too much for her to control. She was no medic. She was just someone doing what she could to save a life. Ripley, therefore, nodded back, recognising that the only chance of survival for that child to have his father was with the individual beside her.

Jodie smiled in agreement. She knew from past encounters like this that it was an unbearable burden to let someone go when you're the person keeping them alive. You feel nothing but responsible for their outcome, no matter how it pans out. Still, she was glad she had agreed on what was right for Singh, regardless of how it made her feel.

"Thank you. I know it hurts, but thank you. You'll lift your hands a tad on three, and my colleague here will take over, pressurising the wound," Jodie said, never once breaking her focus on Ripley.

Though it may not have looked like it, she wanted her to know that she had done everything possible to keep Singh breathing despite his unresponsive state. But aside from that, she also wanted her to understand that if the unthinkable were to occur with Singh, to know it wasn't on her, no matter what she might think in the years to come.

Ripley, in return, stared at Jodie, unable to look away from her innocent smile, trusting the stranger she'd just met with Singh's life, as she graciously nodded in agreement.

"Good, on my count, then. One, two, three, lift."

Once the number left Jodie's lips, Ripley lifted her hands-off Singh's wound, allowing her companion to intervene, maintaining pressure. After that, she got to work taking the tools from her med kit to halt the blood flow and keep him stable.

Ripley slowly got to her feet and exited the living room, heading outside. She wiped her hands all over her clothes, drenching them in blood as she stepped out into the sunlight. Ripley stood on the doorstep, closed her eyes, and took a deep breath. She shut the rest of the world out, all the chaos as her body absorbed the sun's rays. At this moment, she let all her thoughts about what just happened to subside. She chose not to dwell on Singh's state, confident in Jodie's abilities to save him, unlike her own. Ripley held her breath for a couple of seconds before releasing it, allowing her distress to pass over her. After that, she opened her eyes, feeling a sense of familiarity return to her, only for her gaze to be drawn straight to North.

She was right. The wounds she'd inflicted meant North couldn't escape, but that didn't stop him from trying to crawl away. He'd made it what looked like twenty feet down the road, based on the long blood trail behind before the CTSFO had arrived, subduing him. They kept him pinned on the ground, keeping pressure on his various wounds, as they waited for the paramedics. Ripley walked over to him, hand resting on her pistol as the officers around her subconsciously stepped back. They all knew this was the person responsible for murdering and maiming their friends today. None of them would dare intervene if she drew her pistol to shoot him right now. Ripley was the senior officer, and they'd gladly support her decision. They'll make up whatever report was needed to justify her actions. For them, it's justice, making sure this piece of shit didn't get to live a second longer for the pain he'd caused them and their families.

Except it wasn't the kind Ripley wanted. Murdering him like this wouldn't change anything or bring any of their friends back. No matter how easy and how much she wanted to raise her pistol and unload every bullet into him until his heart stopped beating forever, Ripley knew it wasn't true justice. All it would do was plunge her into a dark, inescapable place, perhaps the same one where North lived, where taking life without reason was as natural as breathing.

Ripley wasn't willing to destroy herself over him; he wasn't worth it. He just wasn't. Instead, she raised her hand away from the pistol and stared down, knowing she'd stopped him. He'd spend the rest of his remaining existence in a four-by-four cage for his crimes, and that was justice enough for her.

The end had come. North knew it, laying on the ground, feeling the slither of tears dripping down his cheek. It wasn't from the bullets, but from the utter shame he felt for disgracing the name he'd built. Once those bullets ripped into him, he knew it was over. In his twenty-plus years of killing, he never once sustained an injury like that. This, coupled with the lack of control he'd already experienced since the loft, meant he lost perspective on what was important to him. It wasn't about escaping to live another day but finishing the job. As it was, he lay bleeding out, unable to recall if he'd even shot his last target. It was all one massive blur, but he didn't care anymore. If he lived, it meant nothing, nothing at all. There was no recovering from this indignity or regaining the self-control he once found in that desert so long ago. His life had ended, so he just laid back, closing his eyes, hoping he'd never have to open them again.

The paramedics rushed out at breakneck speed towards the house once the ambulances arrived on the scene. One paramedic, however, stopped dead in her tracks once she saw North bleeding out on the road and the blood-soaked state Ripley was in. She realised they needed attention as well and changed direction to assist them. That was until Ripley intervened, blocking her path.

"No, I need you to check on Singh first. Once he and his family are safe, then and only then can you treat the prick who did it to them. Is that clear?"

The paramedic stared at Ripley, knowing her intention, and nodded back, respecting her decision, before rushing inside to join her colleagues. North was going to live. His wounds were nasty but not fatal, like Singh's. It meant he could wait in pain while the paramedics tried to save his last victim. It's the least he could do considering all the anguish he caused them.

Ripley glanced around, seeing the street closing down as more officers arrived, and realised there wasn't much left for her to do. She, therefore, walked over to the front of the house, dropping and allowing her battered body to take some much needed rest. The mission was complete. After years of murder and destroying lives, North was finally in cuffs. It was over, for good.

Chapter 29

Ripley had cleaned all the bloodstains off her and changed into something fresh as she sat slumped in Denver's office, waiting for him to arrive. After being examined by the medics, she was lucky not to have sustained any lasting injuries from the day's events. There were no broken bones, fractures, or even a mild concussion. She had a few bruises that looked worse than they were but would fade away with time. However, what wouldn't disappear were the latest scars on her body, sustained from pieces of shrapnel slicing across her stomach during the loft blast. It was nothing profound, but it left its mark. It joined her ever-growing collection of scars, but apart from that, she was in good health, physically, at least.

Denver entered his office, gazing at Ripley with admiration for what she'd undergone. In spite of all the bloodshed and carnage she had witnessed to protect one bitter man's career, she rose above all of it. She accomplished something agents with decades more experience had failed to do, including himself in stopping one of British intelligence's biggest disgraces. He made his cheerful way over to his desk, unlocking the bottom drawer. He produced two glasses and a bottle he kept hidden in case of emergency, for those good days when he couldn't wait to toast his team's latest achievement. In reality, though, it was more often reserved for the dark times, when he had to toast the newest person to have given their life for their country, their home.

"I assume you have no issues with Jameson?" he asked, unscrewing the cap.

A slight smile appeared on Ripley's face. "It's fine, chief."

Denver poured her a glass from what bit he had left. It was something Ripley couldn't help but notice as she accepted, taking a small sip as he lifted his own to toast her achievement.

"Considering everything that happened today, a job well done, but on a more personal note, thank you for what you did. You bought peace for a lot of agents today. Well done."

Ripley followed suit, toasting herself. "No worries, chief. Cheers," she muttered as she sipped some more.

Denver sensed something still troubled her from the events of today. He'd seen it happen to over a dozen agents before her and figured he would surely see it on many more before his time in the Section was done. He'd learned from experience that leaving it was never the right call. It always did more harm to their well-being, letting it build and devour them until they slowly cracked.

Denver paced over, settling down beside her. "Do you want to talk about it, or do you just want me to guess?"

A brief smile appeared as Ripley turned to him.

"This entire thing was too close to being a complete disaster. A minute or two later, North would have escaped again, I'm sure of it."

Denver sipped his drink, knowing it was always about the seconds in this job. The difference between life and death for so many individuals out in the field. It's something every agent couldn't escape, thinking about, playing each moment over and over again in their mind. They'll wonder for years if it would have been better if I had done this. If I were faster here, that person wouldn't have escaped, or if I had spent more time here, we would have found that out sooner. It's enough to drive anyone mad, regardless of what they do, but more so in this line of work, where daily failures cause innocent people to die.

"I can't deny it. Today was a more harrowing experience than you had faced so far, but you handled yourself admirably. Due to this, Anil Singh is alive in a hospital bed with his family, safe at his side, as opposed to lying on a slab in a morgue. So, no matter how horrendous this day appears, it didn't turn out as terrible as you think, and that's down to you, and you alone," Denver remarked with pride.

Ripley reluctantly nodded, acknowledging what he said. "Yeah, I know. I'm happy about it. Truly, I am," she said, sipping at her drink, trying to subdue her anguish.

Denver recognised she was still holding something back and was unwilling to let it go. He knew if he didn't at least give it a shot, it would take hold of her like a disease. She'd lose herself in it until there was nothing left to recognise the young women who'd achieved the unthinkable today in apprehending David North.

"Naomi, what is it?" he asked, trying not to impose but feeling like she could talk to him without feeling judged or scrutinised, as a friend.

Ripley paused, taking a deep breath, looking at Denver, knowing she needed to tell him the whole truth. Despite how it made her seem, she needed to tell someone.

"I've never lost people like this before. A lot of people, and I mean a lot, died under my leadership today. Some families lost a child, a sibling, a parent, a cousin or a friend, with countless more still in hospital beds, waiting, in critical condition. They're all dead, or about to be, because they followed me into battle. It's the one thing my father never taught me in our short time together. Like my mother's death, he never understood how to live with the guilt of failing to protect his men, whose screams filled his mind like they do mine. He always hid it from me well, but I knew their deaths hurt him in ways words couldn't explain. I . . . I just don't know how I'm supposed to live with it if he couldn't," she said, taking a deep sip.

Denver remained nothing but calm as he held Ripley's palm to help comfort her.

"This job isn't easy. It never will be because you can't save everyone. It's just not possible. We can't escape it; no matter how hard you try to change it, you just can't. All you can ever do is remember what each individual you lost died for. Only once you learn to acknowledge it does the eternal weight become bearable. Still, take it from someone with experience, dwelling and thinking about how you would do things differently doesn't and will never help. You can't ever alter the past, Ripley; only learn from it."

Ripley gazed with gratitude at Denver for helping to give her some peace of mind. Of course, it didn't stop her from feeling like complete shit, nor did it make the pain any less intense. However, it helped her lighten up to know that it would be alright in some form soon enough. The agony would subside, the screams would fade, and she'd be okay with it. In some sense, she would be okay. Her life would carry on like it always had.

"Thank you," she uttered, downing the rest of her whisky. "On that note, I'll call this a day."

"I'll see you in the morning. Oh, and I recommend taking a day off from running. I think you might have earned a lie-in, so I suggest you take it."

Ripley laughed to herself for what felt like the first time since entering the Section this morning. "I'll think about it, chief, I promise," she said, patting him on the shoulder as she exited the office.

Denver turned to watch her leave, lifting his drink to her as a mark of respect. He realised she was maybe the most remarkable agent he ever had the good fortune to know. He was proud to have someone of her character and moral standard representing his Section.

Ripley exited the building onto the street, beginning her walk home, reflecting on the carnage North caused in the last twenty-two hours. Despite his best efforts, he and his accomplices were all sitting in prison cells. Each of them had played a unique role in the madness that had transpired today, some more than others, but all would answer for their crimes. At best, it would provide the victims' families with some sense of closure. They'll know their grief will not be in vain if nothing else, the murderers responsible for this would never commit these heinous acts against anyone else again. Then, at some point, maybe months or years down the line, they'll be able to find the courage to continue their lives without that loved one. In the same way every other victim has done before them and will continue to do so.

Ripley also reflected on all that happened to her, from each officer she saw murdered in pursuit of one man and everything she'd endured to stop that man's madness. She knew that the pain would never leave her. She'd carry those scars for the rest of her life, along with all the others, for however long it may be. Still, it didn't change the fact that, come tomorrow, she would have to suffer through it all over again, the day after, and so on. It was her job to stop the psychopaths, the extremists, and murderers like David North so that individuals like Anil Singh could be alive with their families.

A job that extended beyond all the anguish and trauma she regularly sustained. It was a privilege for her to perform, for it infused her with a sense of pride and virtue that no other profession could offer. She knew what she did helped make the country she called home that bit safer. It reassured her to know that whatever type of threat or situation might arise tomorrow, the day after or even weeks from now, she'd remain strong.

It doesn't matter how volatile or extreme the circumstances may seem. She was ready to face it head-on, despite how harmful it could be to her.

After all, that was who Ripley was. She was just an ordinary individual, doing what she could to protect her home from the monsters who inhabited it, no matter who they may be.

Acknowledgements

I must start with the entire team at Gatekeeper Press, especially Jamie Anderson, my author manager, who made this process as easy and comfortable as possible. She never rushed me to finish for a deadline that suited her or the company. She instead happily waited for me to finish this at my own pace, which is why this novel is as good as it is, so thank you.

My deepest thanks belong to my editors, Tia Mele, Jessica Knauss, and Jessica Wheaton. Their advice and suggestions allowed me to make this novel the best version of itself while still giving me the freedom to write the story I wanted to tell. They did it by never telling me what to write but by nudging me in the right direction so every sentence would be both grammatically correct and compelling to read.

My sincere thanks to Sandra Dević for creating such a beautiful cover design that embodies the essence of an idea I've lived with for nearly three years. I, however, must thank her even more for her unfailing patience. For every single minuscule detail, I asked her to adjust or show me in a different colour, style, or font so I could get the exact version I wanted.

I want to express my appreciation to my Volvo colleagues, Lady Alexander Page & Ben Holden. They both unknowingly took time out of their day to answer my ridiculous questions about cars. Even though they didn't know what I was on about or what it was for, as I didn't want to give away what I was working on.

Lastly, my most sincere thanks are to Praveen Bhatti, a loving little brother who's supported my creative endeavours all my life, even when no one else was willing to. He was one of the few people who knew I was attempting to write this novel, and at the time, all he said was to go for it. And I'm glad to say I did.

Author Bio

Jay Bhatti is a filmmaker who created the award-winning short film "The Talk" and currently has many other shorts in the pipeline and a feature version of "The Talk" he is trying to raise funds for. Apart from that, he is also an avid film lover who runs a thriving film review channel that has uploaded over five hundred reviews as of this publication. At the time of writing, he is also a successful international parts advisor for his local Volvo dealership, selling to countries in both the Middle East and Oceania. Aside from all that though, he is now an officially published author, eager to bring even more of his ideas to fruition.

If you want to view his film work, type the URL below into your search engine and enjoy.

https://youtu.be/EMlsRE978yc

Lightning Source UK Ltd.
Milton Keynes UK
UKHW020635220223
417437UK00010B/232